# LUCIEN

## THE MARCHESI FAMILY 1

### SILVIA VIOLET

Lucien (Marchesi Family 1) by Silvia Violet

Copyright © 2020 by Silvia Violet

Edited by Susie Selva

Cover Art by Cate Ashwood

Published in the United States of America.

*Lucien* is a work of fiction. Names, places, characters, and incidents are either the product of the author's imagination or are fictionalized. Any resemblance to any actual persons, living or dead, is entirely coincidental.

# 1

## PETER

Peter

I sighed as I pulled open the heavy wooden door of my uncle's bar. After I'd finished yet another day at yet another shit job the temp agency sent me to, I'd wandered aimlessly until I'd ended up there on D Street. Uncle Mac had taken me in at fifteen when my parents had died. He was several years older than my father, and his kids were long grown by then, but he'd done his best by me. I could always count on him for a word of encouragement when I started to doubt I'd ever find my place in the world.

Uncle Mac was behind the bar as usual, busy with the after-work rush. He lifted his chin to acknowledge he'd seen me. I knew as soon as he got a chance he'd make his way down to the end of the bar where I'd settled myself. I wished I could become invisible while I waited. I couldn't be more out of place at the bar in my dress clothes. The fact that I'd gotten them used and they'd seen better days made no difference. I didn't fit in amongst the construction workers and factory linemen or really in South Boston at all.

"Bad day?" My uncle's question pulled me from my thoughts.

"The worst. It's no wonder the man I was working for can't fill his assistant position. He treated me like something a roach would look down on and expected me to do the work of at least three people. Then the son of a bitch had the nerve to say he was going to report my bad attitude to the temp agency and refused to pay me for my day's work."

"You need me to do something about that?" My uncle would literally go beat the man to a pulp for me if I asked him to, but I wouldn't do that.

"No, it's fine. He's just one more in the line of fucking assholes. From what I've heard they've had trouble with him at the agency before, so I don't think they'll pay attention to him. They'll just send me to some new asshole tomorrow while they argue with him about my pay."

"You can always work here. You know that."

I nodded. "I know."

He clapped me on the shoulder. "Don't go anywhere. It's been too long since I've seen you, but I've got to serve these guys before they get rowdy." He jerked his thumb toward a crowd of men who were lined up at the far end of the bar.

Mac would hire me in a second or try to help me find a job working for some friend of his. But I'd never felt comfortable at the bar, and I was pretty sure most of his friends' businesses were far less legal than his own. I'd had enough of trying to lay low, growing up with the parents I'd had. And I'd worked hard to do better for myself. I'd spent two years at community college and earned a scholarship that helped me transfer and finish out my four-year degree. I'd had a good, steady job as an office assistant for two years until the company I worked for downsized and laid me off. Since then, I'd tried to find another assistant position, but none of my temp jobs had developed into more than a few weeks working in shitty conditions. I was twenty-five but I looked younger, and it was hard to get anyone to take me seriously.

Would working for Uncle Mac really be worse than rejection after rejection when I applied for jobs or the horror of the temp work I was assigned? I looked around at the men in the bar. Most of them wore jeans and flannel shirts. Some wore work overalls, and many were still covered with the dirt and dust of their day's work. I had nothing against working hard. I'd taken jobs on a few construction crews, but when you're as small and skinny as me and so obviously gay, that's not a good environment. As a teenager, I'd worked in the back, washing dishes, and I'd been scared to come out front except when the place was nearly empty. I really didn't belong in a Southie bar.

No matter how good or bad any of them were individually, Uncle Mac's regulars were a rough crowd. The more they drank, the louder their opinions got, and the more apt they were to use their fists to make sure everyone knew how right they were. Few of them would be happy being served by a skinny twink who didn't need a rainbow flag to proclaim his orientation. And there were others who would want to shove me to my knees in the back alley and protest that they weren't gay while they shoved their cocks down my throat. I'd only been stupid enough to be lured in by that kind of asshole once.

"Still doing the temp thing?" I turned to see my cousin Jimmy standing behind me. He was the son of my father's other brother, who drank himself to death several years ago. From what Uncle Mac told me about Jimmy's drinking and drug use, he was headed in the same direction. Mac was the best of the lot. I'd been lucky to end up in his care.

"Yep. I just spent a day working for another fucking asshole."

"And you don't even have a drink yet?"

I shook my head. I'd learned early that drinking your problems away was a terrible idea. "I just came by to see Mac."

Jimmy managed to slither his way in between the stool I'd claimed and the large man sitting on the one next to me. The man glared, and Jimmy glared back.

"I've got a proposition for you," Jimmy said.

I resisted the urge to roll my eyes. Jimmy's propositions usually involved us getting high together or me going in on a moneymaking scheme anyone with common sense would know wasn't going to work. "What is it this time?"

"Jesus, don't look at me like that. I've got a job for you. A nice one. In an office. Working for some rich guy."

"If this job is so good, why don't you take it for yourself?"

"I was supposed to, but I got a better offer."

I frowned. "You got a better offer than a steady paying office job?"

"Yeah, from a friend of my dad. He's in sales. If you know what I mean." He winked, and I did roll my eyes then.

"So you're working for a dealer now?"

"Jesus, don't tell the whole bar."

"Jimmy, you're going to get yourself killed."

"No, I'm going to get myself rich."

How could he be so stupid? "What is this job you're talking about, really?"

He fiddled with his phone, not meeting my eyes. "It's just a job. I heard about it through a friend."

"What kind of friend?"

"He owed me a favor, but that doesn't matter. It's exactly the kind of thing you've been looking for."

I knew better than to get my hopes up, but I was fucking desperate. "Is this job legitimate? Tell me the truth."

"It's perfectly legitimate. It's a real company."

I knew better than to believe him, but I couldn't let it go without finding out more. "What would I be doing exactly?"

"You'd be like a secretary"

"An office assistant?"

"Yeah," he waved away my correction. "Whatever the fuck they call it now. Or maybe it was a receptionist. Something like that."

Either position would be way better than my current prospects. "You want me to believe someone offered you this job, and you think they'll just take me instead?"

"Maybe. Maybe not, but if you're willing to do the work, you've at least got a chance."

"When and where were you supposed to show up?" I couldn't believe I was actually considering this.

"Tomorrow morning at nine o'clock. Here." He reached into his jacket, extracted a business card, and handed it to me. "The address is on there."

I pulled out my phone and looked up the company name, Distinguished Properties. They had a nice website, but that didn't mean anything.

"What are you not telling me?" With Jimmy there were always more layers to everything he said.

"Nothing. You're such a suspicious fuck these days."

"I'm suspicious because I know you."

"Look, sometimes I've misrepresented things in the past, but this is a real job. I'm serious."

I wanted to believe that. I wanted it so much I was

tempted to show up and see what happened. I probably would if I were braver, but I was a coward. I hadn't even had the nerve to try and save my parents. When I had the choice of fight or flight, I chose flight every time. I'd learned it was best to keep my head down. I liked how small I was because it was easier for me to stay off people's radars.

"If you really don't like the idea…" It took me a few moments to realize Jimmy was speaking to me again. "… pretty gay boy like you. I could probably find you a sugar daddy, I know a couple of men who—"

"No, Jimmy. Absolutely not." I shuddered at the thought of the kind of men he knew and what they'd expect of me.

"So you'll take the job?"

I shrugged. "Maybe."

"I need to know Petey."

I hated when he called me that. "Why? What does it matter to you if you don't want the job?"

"I just feel bad. They're expecting me to show up, and I'd hate for them to be left in the lurch, ya know?"

There was definitely something Jimmy wasn't telling me. "Why don't you just call and say no thank you. Let them know you found something else."

"My other offer came up last minute, and I didn't want to disappoint the friend who owed me the favor."

"Jimmy, this is—"

"I swear to you. It's a real honest-to-God paying job in an office. Just go."

"If this job is so good—"

"Sorry, got to go. He's a little put out with me right now." He tilted his head toward Mac who was heading our way. When I turned back to say something else to Jimmy, he was gone. I caught a glimpse of him as he disappeared into the crowd.

Mac scowled at Jimmy's retreating back. "That son of a bitch hasn't paid his tab in months, yet he keeps getting the other bartenders to give him drinks."

"If he didn't know how to be charming, he'd probably be dead by now."

Mac huffed. "Fucking asshole."

I started to tell Mac about the job Jimmy wanted me to take, but I thought better of it. Mac would tell me to forget about it and try to convince me to work for him again. I didn't feel like arguing with anyone else. It had been a really long day.

I stepped outside with Mac and talked to him while he took his smoke break, then I gave him a hug and said good night.

As I walked home, I felt weighed down. It was all I could do to lift my feet and keep going. Maybe I should do what Jimmy suggested. I didn't know for sure that he was lying. What if this was my big break? I knew better than to get my hopes up. Most likely, I wouldn't even have the nerve to show up at Distinguished Properties. The best thing to do was head back to the temp agency and hope to be sent someplace where the people were just incompetent rather than vicious.

I sank onto my bed, not even bothering to take my clothes off. Maybe I'd just stay there under the covers. I was so fucking tired. I'd been supporting myself since I was eighteen. There had been some lean times, but I'd always pulled through without having to ask for help. I was proud of that, but sometimes, I wished I had someone who would take care of me or, better yet, a fairy tale prince who would rescue me from the endless day-to-day struggle of trying to find a job and a little respect.

## 2

## LUCIEN

I straightened my tie and gave myself one final look in the mirror. Satisfied with the cut of my new suit and assured I'd exerted my usual level of control over my wavy hair, I went in search of my brother and my cousin. They weren't passed out half-naked in the foyer again, which was something at least. I heard a sound from the dining room, but when I walked in, it was only one of the maids bringing in a chafing dish.

I didn't know why I'd thought Angelo and Devil would be eating at this hour. When I was especially bad as a kid, our mother would send me to wake up Angelo. It was one of my least favorite punishments. And Devil's idea of breakfast was a whiskey and a blow job.

I already wasn't looking forward to this day, and now I had to track down those assholes if I was going to have their backing for a meeting with our allies. I read through some unpleasant messages while enjoying one of the chocolate croissants our housekeeper made especially for me and taking in enough caffeine to face the day. Then I went in search of Angelo and Devil.

I heard laughter coming from Angelo's room and opened the door without knocking. "What the fuck are you two doing in here?"

Angelo was lying sideways across the bed, and Devil was stretched out on the sofa in the sitting area.

The only response I got to my question was more laughter. They were the only people who would dare show me so little respect. "Have you been to bed at all?"

Devil frowned. "I don't think so. Angel, did we go to bed last night?" I still used my brother's full name, but the two of them had been known as Angel and Devil since they were little kids.

Angelo shook his head, then groaned and rolled to his stomach.

"If you're going to puke, get the fuck into the bathroom," I said.

Angelo held up a hand. "I'm good."

"No, you're fucking not. You're both supposed to be ready to go downtown. We've got business to attend to today."

Devil huffed. "You mean Damian Ricci coming after you? That's not business. That's pest control."

"If he were working alone, that's all it would be, and I would've taken care of it without even involving you two idiots, but he's been putting feelers out to anyone with a grudge against us. It's like he's finally realized he needs some strength behind him if he's going to make any kind of move."

"Who would listen to him? He's weak as fuck." Angelo sat up and ran a hand through his disheveled hair. "And he's a fucking moron."

"Ugly as sin too," Devil added.

"While I don't disagree with either of you, he's saying something that's making people listen. We're going to find out what it is, then we're going to track down everyone who's listening to his bullshit and make them sorry."

"Do I get to do the making them sorry part?" Devil asked.

"Possibly, but you need to prove you can follow the rules this time."

"We haven't gotten where we are by being reckless," Angelo said in a voice that was clearly meant to mock my own. "Come on, Luce. What's the point of all this power if we can't have a little fun with it?"

I started to speak but Devil held up his hand. "Wait. I've got this. If we have too much fun, we'll lose all our power."

"If you two keep joking around, you will lose it right fucking now." I'd thought I was ready to take over the reins of the family business when my father said it was time for him to retire, but at times like this, when the only two men whose loyalty I've never doubted acted like fucking toddlers, I wanted to call my dad back from his months-long vacation and walk the fuck away.

"You know we love you, right, Luce?" Angelo said.

"I know I hate when you call me that. If you two assholes don't sober up and get downtown in the next hour, I'll call Nonna and tell her we just had an interesting chat, and you two are ready to find some nice girls and settle down with them."

Angelo's eyes went wide, and his mouth fell open. "You wouldn't!"

Devil started laughing so hard he fell off the couch. Technically, he was our cousin on my mother's side, and Nonna—my father's mother—wasn't his grandmother, but that hadn't ever stopped her from treating him like her own son. Devil's mother was disinterested at best, malicious at worst. Fortunately, she spent most of her time on another continent. A lot of people mistook Angelo and Devil—whose real name was more or less a family secret—for twins. They were gorgeous and charming and much too used to getting anything they wanted. As far as I was concerned, they were a lot of fucking trouble, but I loved them. If anybody else said a word against them in my presence, they never made that mistake again.

As if by magic, Angelo and Devil managed to look polished and wide-awake by the time we needed to head downtown. I wondered if they would ever get too old to pull off that transition. At thirty-two, I already felt like I was. They were only two years younger than me but didn't have the weight of running the family business on their shoulders.

The meeting with several of our allies was taking place at Distinguished Properties, the commercial real estate business we used as a cover for several of our other enterprises. We took the elevator up to my office. When the door slid open, I expected to see the little snake Jimmy sitting behind the reception desk, waiting to do my bidding. He'd once again failed to pay my family what he owed us. Out of respect for his late father's loyalty to me, I'd given him the chance to work off his debt. While I doubted he'd make much of a receptionist, he at least knew how to be charming and put people at ease. And if he were in my office, he wouldn't be getting himself in more trouble.

But Jimmy wasn't there. Instead, a shockingly beautiful blond-haired twink sat at the reception desk. My brother didn't look a thing like an angel, except maybe the fallen kind who would lead you straight to hell, but this boy looked like the sort of ethereal creature who would guide you to heaven after a hero's death. He looked up at me with bright hazel eyes. "May I help you, sir?"

"You can sure as hell help me," Devil said, propping a hip on the edge of the boy's desk.

I didn't even know the kid's name, but jealousy sizzled

through me. I kicked my cousin's shin. "Get the fuck off the desk, and quit acting like some kind of animal."

"Jesus," Devil said rubbing his leg. "Those shoes you love are fucking lethal."

Angelo held out his hand to my new receptionist. "I'm Angelo, and you're very clearly not Jimmy."

The boy tentatively lifted his hand. Instead of shaking it, Angelo brought it to his lips.

"Back off," I growled. "Where the fuck is Jimmy, and who are you?"

The boy's eyes widened, and color rose in his cheeks. "Jimmy got another offer, and he asked me if I wanted to come here in his place. Ms. Carla said it would be all right for me to have a trial day since there wasn't anyone else here to do the job."

Carla was my assistant, and I would be having words with her very soon. His voice shook so badly I was surprised he'd been able to get that many words out. He looked away as soon as he finished speaking and began to fidget with the pen on his desk.

"Jimmy got another offer?" I looked toward my brother.

Angelo shrugged. "I've not heard a thing."

I looked back at the boy. I could see his pulse fluttering against the pale skin of his neck.

I wanted to run my tongue over it.

I wanted to see him quiver like that underneath me.

I wanted to make him beg.

But before I could consider any of that, I needed to know who he actually was and why Jimmy had sent him to me.

"In my office. Now." I gestured toward my office door.

"Sir, I'm sorry. I asked Jimmy if—"

"First lesson. Don't believe a fucking word out of

13

Jimmy's mouth. Now do what I said. I'm not a man who repeats himself."

Slowly, the boy pushed his chair back, came around his desk, and—seeming to try to keep as much distance between us as possible—moved past me and headed toward my office. I turned to Angelo and Devil. "You two jackasses wait in the conference room. Don't cause me any more trouble. I've got enough to deal with today."

They must've realized I wasn't going to put up with any more of their shit. Angelo shoved at Devil, and they got moving.

"Try not to make him piss himself. I don't want to have to clean that up," Carla said as I walked by her desk. I snarled at her, but she didn't even flinch. Carla was possibly even less afraid of me than my brother and my cousin, but she'd earned it. No one was a better assistant than she was, despite her not calling to let me know Jimmy hadn't shown up. She knew what I needed even before I did.

"I'll be talking to you about this situation when I'm through with him."

"He's got experience as an office assistant," she said. "And I liked him."

I ignored her and followed the boy into my office, my gaze lingering on the perfectly round globes of his ass. I wished to hell I didn't have pressing business. Taking him over my desk would be a much better way to start the day than a fucking meeting where I'd have to posture the whole fucking time.

I closed the door behind me with a firm click and watched my little twink jump. Knowing he was afraid of me turned me on even more.

"Turn around."

He obeyed instantly. I liked that. A lot. "What is your name?"

"Pete. Peter."

"Full name."

"Peter Kelly."

He shivered when I gave him a very obvious once-over. Fuck, I wanted him. "So Pete Kelly, how do you know Jimmy?"

"He's my cousin, sir."

"Do you work with Jimmy?"

He shook his head, a look of disgust on his face. "No, sir. I try to stay away from everything Jimmy is involved in."

"Everything except showing up in my office."

He sighed and looked down at his feet. "I've been out of work for a while. I've been trying to get jobs through a temp agency, but that's not gone well. Jimmy said he had a job for me. I guess I was…"

I watched him for a moment, head bowed, hands clasped in front of him, the perfect picture of surrender. He would surrender to me, but I needed more information first.

"Were you desperate, Peter?"

He didn't respond, but he looked up. The fear in his eyes made my cock begin to fill. I suspected he didn't know much about me, but he knew I was dangerous. "Did Jimmy tell you who I am?"

"He said you were the owner of this business."

I nodded. "That's true, but I feel like that doesn't give you the whole picture. My name is Lucien Marchesi."

His eyes went wide, and he took a small step back. I'd been accused of murdering a young woman several months ago, and the case had gotten a lot of press. I had killed before, and I've ordered others to do it, but I didn't kill that woman. I didn't even know her. Some enemies of mine thought they could set me up. I'd tracked down most of them and made sure that wouldn't be a problem again, but I had a suspicion Damian Ricci was in contact with the ones who had eluded me.

"Are you… I mean…"

"The head of a crime family? Yes. The man who killed that girl? No."

Peter didn't say anything else. He just watched me warily, not that I blamed him. "Did Jimmy tell you why he'd been offered this job?"

Peter licked his lips before he answered. I barely heard his words as I thought about how much better his lips would look wet with my cum. "He said someone owed him a favor."

That fucking son of a bitch. "That was a lie. He owes me a debt. A debt he was paying off by working for me, but…" Peter's hands were clasped so tightly his knuckles had gone white. As if that wasn't enough to betray his nerves, he tapped his foot against the floor in a fast rhythm, though I wasn't sure he even realized it. "Look at me, Peter."

He glanced up, and I watched his throat work as he swallowed.

"I will allow you to work the debt off for him."

# 3

## PETER

I made the mistake of looking into Lucien's eyes again. His gaze held me there. His blue eyes were as dark as the ocean at midnight, and they mesmerized me. He watched me like he wanted to devour me, and I had a feeling he wasn't talking about working off Jimmy's debt employed as his receptionist.

"No thank you. I'll just go. I didn't understand the situation. Jimmy never said anything about... He just said he wasn't taking the job because he'd gotten a better offer."

Mr. Marchesi didn't say anything, so I took a few steps toward the door.

"I didn't dismiss you." His harsh tone froze me in place.

I turned back to face him and tried to remember how to breathe. I had to stay calm if I was going to talk my way out of this. "I appreciate the opportunity, sir, but—"

"I'm not offering you an opportunity. I'm telling you you're staying. A debt needs to be paid, and intentionally or not, you've agreed to take Jimmy's place."

"But he—"

"Lied to you. And he will be dealt with. Don't worry

about that. I'll make sure the work he does for me isn't nearly as pleasant as the job I'm giving you."

Why had I ever listened to Jimmy? I'd known something was wrong. Powerful men didn't just offer assistant jobs to anyone. "Thank you, but I—"

"I'm going to give you the benefit of the doubt, because until now, you didn't know who I was. I don't take no for an answer. When I want something, I get it, and I want you."

"You want *me*, sir? Me?"

He glanced around the room making a show of checking under his desk and behind me. "I don't see anyone else here, so yes, I must be talking to you."

I squeezed my hands into fists, not wanting him to see they were shaking. I might not be the smartest guy, based on the fact that I listened to Jimmy, but I'd have to be a fool not to know Mr. Marchesi was a predator, and I was nothing but a frightened mouse. He spoke with such certainty. I had no doubt he was used to getting what he wanted, and while I didn't know much about designer labels, I could tell his suit fit him like it was tailored for him. His shoes looked like someone had spent hours polishing them. His dark hair was expertly styled, his skin flawless. He had the money to make anything happen. And the way he held himself perfectly still echoed his power. He didn't fidget. He didn't blink. He sized me up, and when I shivered under his gaze, I saw the barest hint of a smile. He liked that I was afraid.

I needed to get away from him, yet it wasn't just fear that had my heart racing, because while I knew he was scary as hell, I also knew he could protect me if he chose. The weight of his presence and his air of utter authority made me crave the chance to learn more about him, and God knows, the man was gorgeous. He'd been created to be as beautiful as he was dangerous, and he wanted me. As stupid as it was, knowing that made my heart flutter. Maybe I really was an idiot because there was no doubt this man could destroy me if he chose. "That's... very flattering, sir, but—"

Mr. Marchesi took a step toward me, then another until he was so close I could reach out and touch him if I dared. I didn't.

"Once you crossed that threshold"—he gestured toward the door to his office—"you became mine. The faster you accept that, the easier things will be for you."

Had his voice really gotten lower and huskier, or was that my imagination? There was heat in his eyes. I was sure of that. They'd been cold before when he'd been angry that Jimmy had sent me, but now they seemed warm, almost comforting, though his words were not.

"You can't own me, sir. No one can."

He shook his head. "You're wrong about that." He reached out and ran the backs of his fingers along my cheek. I sucked in my breath as I shivered again. "You're new to my world. Innocent. So I'll be lenient, but I do not permit defiance from anyone who works for me."

"I don't—" He laid a finger against my lips. I wanted to draw the digit into my mouth and suck on it. What was wrong with me? I needed to find a way out of there. Would he really hold me against my will? I knew something was off when Jimmy sent me here. I knew the job was too good to be true.

"Do you understand what it means when I say you're mine?"

"I... I don't know." But I thought I actually did, and it made me want him when I should have been terrified. I'd hidden from danger and conflict ever since that night when... I pushed the memories away. They still had the power to make me sick, and I needed to focus so I could find a way out of this.

"Kneel." Mr. Marchesi pointed to the floor in front of him.

No, this wasn't happening. I glanced toward the door. It seemed much farther away than it had moments before. I doubted I could outrun him, and he had men outside the door anyway. I wouldn't be able to get away from them, and while Mr. Marchesi wasn't as big as they were, I was certain he was stronger than me. Fuck. He was watching me, like a cat waiting for a mouse to make a move before he pounced.

When I didn't move, he cupped my chin. Heat raced through me as his fingers pressed into my skin, firm but not hard enough to hurt. "I don't give commands a second time."

He let go, and I went to my knees, heart racing. This was wrong, and yet, looking up and seeing his lips curve up in approval made my cock start to swell.

"See. That wasn't so difficult." He held out a hand, palm up.

"Wh-what do you want, sir?" I hated how my voice trembled, but at least my fear was justified this time. Mr. Marchesi was the kind of man who would scare almost anyone.

"Your hand."

I frowned. "I don't—"

"Your hand, Peter." Why did my name sound so sexy on his lips?

I laid my trembling hand over his, and he pulled me to my feet. "Aren't you going to make me…"

"Do you want me to make you?"

I shook my head. "No, sir."

He ran a finger over my lower lip, pressing until I opened my mouth slightly. "Are you sure?"

It was one thing to be forced into taking this job, but to be… I didn't want that, did I?

"I don't need you to do anything else today. I simply needed to prove a point."

"That you're scary?"

He gave me a true smile then, and it made him even more beautiful. "I've proven that you will obey me."

"You didn't give me a choice."

"Is that true, Peter? Did I threaten you?"

"Maybe not technically, but—"

"Did I hold a gun to your head?"

"There are guards outside the door."

"Who are there to protect me. Did I say they would prevent you from leaving?"

He'd implied it. He'd said he always got what he wanted, and… he had. I'd done what he asked and part of me had fucking wanted to.

He smiled as if reading my thoughts. "So now I know you'll do what I ask. As long as you remember what I expect from you, you and I will have a lot of fun together."

"What do you mean exactly?"

He laughed, the sound unexpected. "You might be the most innocent man to ever enter this office, but I think even you can figure that out. You know what I want to do to you, and I don't think you're going to fight me." His gaze ran over my body until he was looking at my erection pressing against the front of my pants. The room wavered. I needed to run, but I was too scared to move.

When our eyes met again, he held my gaze. I felt my rapid heartbeat pulsing in my ears, and the edges of my vision began to darken.

He clapped a hand on my shoulder, steadying me. "I'm a scary man, Peter, but you have no reason to fear me as long as you do what I ask."

What he was asking was wrong. So very wrong. He stepped away suddenly, and I wavered.

"Easy. Take a breath."

I did, obeying him without even thinking about it.

"That's better. I want you to get some water in the lobby before you leave. Be back here at nine tomorrow morning. You'll be here until six at least. I have a lot for you to do."

"Wait. You really are hiring me as your receptionist?"

He gave a slight nod. "I already told you that."

"But I thought…"

"Goodbye, Mr. Kelly. I have work to do."

Somehow I managed to leave his office without tripping over something or passing out. When I passed by a water fountain in the lobby, I stopped and drank from it, just as I'd been commanded. Then I walked out, grateful for once for the cold since the sting of it snapped me out of the spell Lucien Marchesi had me under. I wasn't going to obey any more of his commands. I wasn't going back there. I didn't belong in his world. I wasn't a plaything he could own, and I knew better than to think I would ever be anything more to him. Danger was something I ran from, not to. I'd learned to keep my head down and stay out of trouble, and that's what I would continue to do.

*I want you, and I always get what I want.*

Would he come looking for me if I didn't show up the next day?

No, surely not. He was a busy man. He'd enjoyed toying with me, but I couldn't possibly be that important to him. When I didn't show up, he'd find someone else to play with if he hadn't already forgotten me by then.

———

The next day, I felt even more depressed than usual as I walked to yet another temporary work assignment. I should've been thankful the agency hadn't listened to the asshole I'd worked for two days ago, but all I could think about was Lucien. Jimmy had called me several times the night before, but I'd erased the messages he'd left without listening to them. I wasn't going to let him involve me in his problems any more than he already had. I didn't know what kind of trouble he was in, but if it involved Lucien and his family, it was serious.

I was doing the right thing by not going back. I knew that, but I couldn't help being a little disappointed I wouldn't get to see Lucien again. I didn't want to work for a man like him, and I would never intentionally take a risk like that. I should have been thankful I'd gotten away, but Lucien's presence was so electrifying. I would never know what he might've done to me. The night before, I'd dreamed about him… more than once. In the dreams, he'd put his hands on me and hadn't let me go. He'd expected exactly what I'd thought he would when he made me kneel in front of him. And I'd given him everything he'd asked for and begged for more, then woken up gasping for breath, sweaty, and hard as an iron bar.

I'd never found hookups satisfying, so I'd gotten used to not having anything touch my dick but my own hand. Last night, it hadn't seemed like enough. I zoned out on the red line having slept only fitfully after waking from my dreams of Lucien.

When I exited the train at my stop, I pulled out my phone to check the directions once again. As I studied the map, thick fingers closed around my bicep so hard I yelped. I started to pull away, but another hand came down on my shoulder. I realized there were two men behind me. Two large, broad-shouldered, beefy men I had little chance of getting away from.

"What do you want?" I hated how my voice shook.

"Mr. Marchesi sent us," the man on my right said. "You're late for work."

"He likes everyone to be on time," the other man said.

"Thank you, but I told him I didn't need the job."

The man on my right jerked my arm. "You'll have to tell him that again in person because he asked us to bring you to him."

My heart was racing, and I was afraid I was either going to faint or throw up. But there was a tiny part of me that liked the fact that Lucien didn't want to let me go. I hated myself for even thinking that way.

"Start walking to the car," the man on my left said, gesturing toward a black car illegally parked down the street.

I considered my options. I wasn't going to be able to get away from these men. I'd told myself again and again I should take a self-defense class, but my strategy of hiding from trouble had worked for me so far. Fucking Jimmy.

Would being under Lucien's control be so bad? Images from my dream flashed into my mind.

I shouldn't be thinking that way, but what was I supposed to do? I didn't have any option but to head toward the car like the man had said. Maybe later I could find a way to escape. Maybe Lucien wouldn't turn out to be as bad a man as I thought.

Yeah, right. Like I would be that lucky.

# 4

## LUCIEN

"Mr. Marchesi?" Carla called over the intercom.

"Yes?"

"Leo and Rick are here with your new receptionist."

"Send Peter in, and do not let anyone disturb me for any reason."

"Yes, sir."

I looked up from my desk when the door opened a few seconds later. I heard Carla whisper "Go on" before Peter took a tentative step toward the doorway and then another one.

"Close the door behind you and lock it," I said looking back down at the papers in front of me.

"Sir, please. I—"

"I didn't ask you to speak. Come stand in front of my desk."

I saw him move in my peripheral vision, but I deliberately didn't look at him. I took my time reviewing the reports I'd been looking over. When I was done, I closed my leather folio, folded my hands on top of it, and gave Peter a slow perusal, letting him see my displeasure. "I told you to be here at nine o'clock. Did you misunderstand me?"

He shook his head. "No, sir. I didn't think it was a good idea to come back."

"You know what's not a good idea, Peter? Disobeying me. When I tell a man to do something, he does it or faces the consequences."

"Consequences, sir?"

"Did you honestly think that you could just not show up for your job and… what? I wouldn't notice? I wouldn't care?"

"I thought… I didn't really think you wanted me to work for you. You wanted Jimmy—"

"I don't want Jimmy for anything. Jimmy is a piece of shit. I was doing Jimmy a favor, but now he's lost his chance with me. You, on the other hand, I wanted. I made that very clear." I rose and started to move around the desk.

Peter took a step back.

"Don't move."

He drew in a shaky breath, but he stayed where he was. I moved behind him, intentionally keeping him on edge.

"Do you know what the consequences are for disobeying me?"

"P-please don't hurt me. I'm sorry. I'll work for you. I'll do whatever you say."

"That's right. You will," I said, stepping so close he could feel my breath on his neck. I saw the fine hairs stand up as I blew against them. Peter shivered.

"I'm afraid I can't promise the consequences won't hurt, but there won't be any permanent damage."

"Please, give me another chance."

"No, Peter. I need you to understand how very serious I am when I ask you to do something."

"I know now."

"Do you? Do you know what I want from you, Peter?"

"N-no."

"Everything," I said the word in a low voice right by his ear, and I dropped my hand to the gorgeous curve of his ass. "When you're disobedient, you'll get punished. It will be my hand today, but if you refuse to follow my orders again, it will be my belt or maybe even the cane."

"You're going to spank me?" He shivered again as I ran a hand down his back and cupped his ass once more.

"I am. Drop your pants and brace yourself on the desk."

"You can't just—"

I wrapped a hand around his throat, caressing him with my thumb. "I can do anything I want. You came to me, and I decided to keep you."

"I didn't know. Jimmy told me—"

I blew against his neck once more, then traced the outer edge of his ear with my tongue. "You should always investigate future employers."

"Please. I don't want trouble."

"Then you should've been on time for work today." I rested my hands against his waist and felt him exhale. Then I kissed him over the rapid pulse that had intrigued me the day before. He whimpered when I flicked it with my tongue, and if I hadn't already decided he was mine, that sound would have made me claim him.

"Wh-what if someone comes in?" I doubted he knew he'd given himself away, but his words let me know he'd accepted his punishment as inevitable.

"No one would dare." I bit the soft skin of his neck gently. He sucked in his breath and tilted his head, exposing more of his neck to me. "That's it. Surrender to me. It will be easier that way."

"Please." This time, I suspected he was asking for more rather than begging for mercy. I reached for his belt buckle, undid it, and then unbuttoned his pants and lowered his zipper. He shuddered as I pressed my palm into the hard length of his cock. I was right. He wanted this.

"Do you need a man who will demand obedience from you, Peter?"

"No, I… I don't know."

"I think you do. I'm going to be that man for you. I'm going to control you, but I'm also going to take care of you." I let go of him and stepped back. "Now drop your pants and hold on to the edge of my desk."

His hands went to his fly but then he hesitated. "I already know you will obey. It's only a matter of how long you make me wait. The longer that is, the harsher your punishment. This is going to happen. I'm going to redden your ass, show you how serious I am, and then for the rest of the day, you're going to go out there and do your job."

"A-and after that?"

The tremble in his voice made me even harder. I'd be lucky to get anything done for the rest of the day because I wasn't going to fuck him. Not yet. Not here. The first time I had the pleasure of sliding into his gorgeous ass, I was going to take my time.

"You're going to come back to work tomorrow, and you're going to do as you're told." I didn't think this was the time to announce that he would also be moving into my house. My investigation of his life had shown me his apartment was unsafe, and my enemies were too restless to leave him unpro-tected. I could keep a guard on him, but it would be so much easier—and more pleasurable—if he were under my roof.

A few more seconds passed. I watched his shoulders rise

and fall gently with his breaths. Then he pushed his pants and boxer briefs down his legs. A man with less control than me would've groaned at the sight. I wanted to bury my face against his ass, to lick, to savor, but there would be time for that later.

Slowly, he reached out his arms and grasped the edge of the desk.

"That's good, Peter. See how easy it is to obey?"

A small sound escaped him, and it made me long to hear more. But not here. Carla and anyone else who'd witnessed him being sent to my office would know I intended to punish him, but his cries were for me, not them.

"You're going to have to keep quiet. Can you do that?"

"I don't know."

He was so honest. Was he as innocent as he seemed? If so, he absolutely needed my protection.

"Try your best. I'll gag you if I have to."

"I—"

I cracked my hand against his ass. He jumped, but he didn't cry out.

I didn't give him time to think before I spanked him again and then kept going. He whined and whimpered and dropped down to his elbows on the desk. His ass was even more gorgeous with my handprint across it, and my cock was begging to be freed. Just thinking of the way Peter would react to me pushing into him, fucking him deep, was making me crazy.

I slapped the reddest part of his ass harder than I had before. This time, he yelped. I clamped a hand over his mouth. "I need you quiet."

I used my other hand to give him several blows in rapid succession. He tried to pull away from me, so I let go of his mouth and pushed him down flat against my desk, not caring when papers went flying. "I'm not finished yet."

"Please. It hurts, please."

"I want it to hurt. I want you to remember how this feels any time you think about disobeying my orders. Do you understand?"

He whimpered. "I expect an answer."

"Yes, sir." He exhaled, and I felt him relax against the desk. I'd been right. Control was exactly what he needed.

5
___

## PETER

My ass was on fire. It hurt like hell, but it wasn't like any pain I'd felt before. It heated me up, electrified me, and made me so hard I was afraid I was going to come as his hand came down on my ass again and again. I wanted to make it stop, but I also wanted to beg him to keep going. What was wrong with me? I should've been angry, scared, and humiliated by what he was doing to me, but I fucking loved it.

I struggled to breathe through my nose as his hand clamped hard against my mouth. I'd tried to be quiet, but how could I when he sent pain singing through me as he made me hurt, made me want.

I felt near my breaking point, ready to cry or scream or fight as a riot of emotions and confusion churned inside me. Then he hit me so hard pain blazed through my whole body. I struggled, suddenly desperate to get away. He shoved me down over the desk. I protested, but he wouldn't relent. He demanded my surrender.

As he held me there against the cool, hard surface, his hand caressed my sore ass. Something in me did break, but not like I'd expected it to. I didn't try to shove him off me. I didn't fight. I gave in, and it felt incredible. I was sure I would be angry with myself later, but right then, I accepted it. This was what I needed. Dominance. Control. Clear expectations. "Please, I need…"

"I know what you need."

He smacked my ass again and again. I was so hot, so needy. I knew it hurt, but the pain felt far away somehow. I arched my back, reaching my ass toward his hand. My cock was so hard. If I could just get some friction…

Lucien spanked me hard enough to push me farther across the desk. A cry escaped me, and he slid a hand into my hair, gripping it tight and turning my head so I faced him.

"You're mine, and I expect your obedience."

"Yes, sir." The words were out before I had time to think about them or consider what I was agreeing to.

He gripped my hips, yanking me back from the desk. I slid along the surface, crumpling papers, but he seemed oblivious to that.

He reached under me, and his hand circled my cock. "You're going to come for me now. Your body knows what it needs. I can give you pain, but I can also give you pleasure. So much pleasure."

His strokes were slow, and his grip not tight enough. "Please. Please, I need…"

His hand tightened in my hair again. "Tell me what you need."

"To come."

"I can tell. You're leaking so much, I bet there's a puddle of precum on the floor. Should I make you lick it up when I'm done with you?"

I sucked in my breath. The thought of that shouldn't be hot. It was humiliating. It was wrong. "No, please."

He laughed, the sound rich and dark. "You would do it if I ordered you to."

I didn't bother to protest because I was sure I would. He'd proven I would obey him. I'd kneeled for him, bared my ass to him, let him hurt me, and liked it. What wouldn't I do?

"What else do you want?"

"I… I don't know."

"Yes, you do"

I swallowed hard. I knew a lot of things I wanted, but I didn't want to admit to them. He teased a single finger along the length of my cock. I needed so much more.

"Tell me."

"This. You. Whatever you're doing to me, I…"

"That's right. You need everything I want to do to you."

Lucien stepped back, and I bit my lower lip to hold in a protest as he yanked on my hair, jerking me upward. I pressed my hands against the desk to lever myself up as he pulled me back against him. Then he spun me to face him. His eyes were even darker, nearly black now, the pupils huge. At least I knew he was affected by this too. I glanced down and saw his cock pressed against his tight suit pants.

"Fuck yes, I'm hard for you," he said. "I love the feel of you surrendering to me. Now look at me."

I was scared to look up and see the intensity in his eyes because I wanted to tell him he could have me. I wanted to give in, not just to his punishment, to everything. I knew that was crazy. There was no telling what evil he'd done. I didn't know if he'd killed that woman or not, but I didn't think he was a man who would hesitate to kill if he wanted to.

He gripped my chin, forcing me to meet his gaze. His fingers squeezed me so hard I wondered if there'd be bruises along my jaw. He eased up the pressure once our eyes met, and his other hand reached for my cock again. "Hold your shirt up out of the way. Mine won't fit you, and I haven't had a chance to get anything in your size to keep in my office. I can't have my receptionist going around all day with cum stains on his clothes."

I did as he said, pulling my shirt up and folding it over. It would be wrinkled but not stained. What did he mean he intended to order clothes in my size? How did he even know my size? All concern for that vanished when his hand wrapped around my cock again, gripping me tighter this time.

My eyes started to flutter closed, but Lucien's grip on my chin tightened again. "I want you looking at me as I bring you off. I want you to remember who's touching you, who owns you."

I wanted to protest, but he was stroking me faster now, his hold so tight it was just on the edge of painful. I tried to stay still, but I couldn't. My hips seemed to move on their own as I tried to thrust my cock into his hand.

"Go ahead and fuck my hand. I love seeing how much you need this."

I was close. So close. But I was almost scared that if I let go, he would see even deeper into me as he watched, and I was afraid that once I let him bring me off, I would truly be his. I didn't have a choice though, did I? He'd taken that away from me. That should scare me instead of making me feel so fucking free.

"That's it, baby. I know you're right there. Who's giving you this, making you feel so fucking good?"

"You are, sir."

"That's right, so show me how much you love this."

He let go of my chin and squeezed my ass, fingers digging into the sore flesh. That pain was enough to push me over the edge. I nearly bit through my lip to keep from crying out as cum shot from my cock, the pleasure of it rocketing through me. Lucien kept stroking me, and my climax seemed to go on and on, longer than it ever had.

When he finally let go, my knees buckled. I had to reach for the desk to stay on my feet. Lucien pulled tissues from a box on his desk and wiped off his hands. Horrified that I might have ruined his suit, I looked him up and down, but he looked as pristinely put together as ever.

"Over eagerness cost me to ruin a suit once," he said. "I've never let that happen again."

Of course he would magically be able to keep himself looking perfect when I probably looked as used as I felt.

He tossed the tissues in his trash can.

"I have a meeting to get to. Clean yourself up in my washroom." He inclined his head toward the door to his left. "There's an iron in the linen closet if you need it for your shirt."

I stared at him. He hadn't come. "You didn't... I thought..."

"When I fuck you for the first time, it's going to be somewhere private so I can enjoy every sound you make and take as much time as I'd like."

"But aren't you—"

"I've learned how to deny myself and wait for what I want because I know eventually, I'll have everything I've ever desired."

He slipped out the door then, leaving me standing there with my pants around my ankles, sticky with cum and sore from his punishment, but I hadn't missed the fact that he barely opened the door, making certain no one could see in.

*That's because he thinks you're his property, and he doesn't want to share you with anyone else.*

Or was it because he was protecting me? No, I couldn't

let myself imagine him having tender feelings. I hitched my pants up and hobbled into the bathroom.

It was far larger than the one in my apartment and much more richly decorated. There was a stack of washcloths in a basket on the counter. I took one, cleaned myself up, then placed it in the basket that seemed to be for dirty linen. I tucked my shirt back in. I probably should iron it as Lucien had suggested, but I didn't trust my shaky hands to hold an iron. As unsettled as I was, I'd likely burn a hole in it.

When I had my pants fastened, I finally let myself really look in the mirror. My hair was sticking up at crazy angles, my cheeks were bright pink, and my lower lip was puffy from where I'd bitten it again and again as I'd done my best not to be too loud. Had Lucien's assistant and the others in the office heard me? Did they know what he'd done? I didn't think he'd be shy about staking his claim on me.

*I own you.*

How the fuck had I gotten myself into this, and what could I do about him expecting me back tomorrow?

*When I fuck you for the first time, it's going to be somewhere private.*

Was there any chance I could get away from him? Anything I could say to change his mind?

Not after the way I'd responded to him this morning. I certainly couldn't convince him I didn't want him because I did. My body did at least, but I was afraid of him—of his power, of his ability to just take over my life and make demands. He hadn't hesitated to spank me until my ass burned. What else would he do to me if I disobeyed?

He'd mentioned his belt and a cane. That sounded scary as fuck.

My instincts told me he hadn't lied when he said he'd never damage me and that he wouldn't force me to do anything I didn't want. I would never have asked for him to spank me, but I'd enjoyed every second of it.

I didn't belong in this world, though. I belonged somewhere I could live a quiet life, a place where I didn't have to confront my fears, where no one expected anything more than adequacy from me.

I pressed the heels of my hands to my eyes. I would not cry. I might not be strong. I might not be brave. But somehow I was going to walk out there, sit behind my desk, and make Lucien proud. In that moment, pleasing him was what I wanted. Maybe it was time to stop just surviving and enjoy myself. Or maybe I'd end up discarded by him and dead in a ditch. For now at least, I didn't have a choice but to obey him.

# 6

## LUCIEN

$C$arla attempted to get my attention when I left my office, but I walked right past her. I pushed open my brother's office door, not in the mood to knock. He glanced up from where he was working or more likely pretending to work. "Lucien, what the fuck?"

I didn't answer. I just stepped into his bathroom and shut the door. I needed to wash the scent of Peter off my hands. Obviously, I could've used my own bathroom, but I needed to get away from him before my resolve broke. If I'd stayed one more minute, if I'd taken Peter into the bathroom to clean him up myself, I would've fucked him no matter who was around. I told him I'd honed my control, and that was true. My life demanded it. But something about him was pushing me to my limits. I turned on the cold water and stuck my hands under it, needing to feel something that wasn't the heat of my desire for that gorgeous boy. The way he looked as he came, the ecstasy on his face…. It had been years since I'd come in my pants, but I'd been fucking close then.

"Lucien!" Angelo banged on the door. "What the fuck are you doing?"

"Using your fucking bathroom, moron. Back off."

By the time I stepped out into my brother's office, my hard-on was gone, and my control was fully back in place. "It's time for our meeting. Let's go."

"Why are you in here?" Angelo asked. "And why the fuck didn't you knock?"

"I own this building. I don't have to knock."

"Don't try that imperious shit with me."

"That's a big word for you. Better be careful how you throw that around."

He flipped me off. "What was wrong with your bathroom?"

"I needed a change of scenery."

Angelo grinned. "You got that little twink in there? The new receptionist? What did you do? Fuck him until he passed out, then leave the scene of the crime?"

I grabbed the front of Angelo's shirt and slammed him against the wall. "Don't ever speak about Peter like that again. In fact, don't speak about him at all."

Angelo raised his brows. "Damn. I've never seen you like this over a man."

"I want this one to myself."

Angelo whistled, and I'd never regretted more how impossible it was for me to intimidate him or how easily he read me. He was right. This wasn't normal for me. I rarely felt possessive of the men I fucked, and I rarely had the same man twice. I wasn't sure why Peter was different, and that made me uneasy. I didn't want to talk about this, not even with Angelo.

"Don't push me on this, Angelo."

He must've seen something in my expression that made him realize how serious I was.

He brought up a hand and cupped my face. "If you need

to talk, you tell me, okay?"

I nodded. "I'm good."

"Stay that way."

I let him go and stepped back. "We're late, and I need you to behave in there."

Angelo grinned. "Always."

"Liar." He fucking never acted like he took anything seriously. I knew better. He was listening, absorbing everything that was said even as he joked around until everyone was ready to kill him.

Everyone else was already there when we arrived: Devil, Vincent Trevisani, the son of one of my father's closest allies, Vinnie was slowly taking control of the family, but this was the first time I'd worked with him directly.

We'd also invited Stefan Romano, another member of an allied family. He was Angelo's age, but he'd often hung out with me and his older brother, Ash, which had been awkward since Ash and I were a hell of a lot more than friends though very much in the closet.

Next to him at the table was Marco Ricci, Damian's estranged nephew. I had serious reservations about trusting him. He'd argued with his uncle years ago, thinking their business should go a new direction. After being disowned, he'd set himself up as a fence, and we'd worked with him occasionally. He came to me asking to help take down his uncle, but a few days ago, Stefan had heard a rumor that Marco had been sniffing around his uncle again trying to make amends. Maybe he just wanted info or maybe he wanted to bring us down. I was watching him, but I had every intention of using him to get the information we needed.

Devil had also insisted we include a couple of men he liked to use for muscle who'd worked for the Riccis and been screwed over. The Riccis still owed them for a big job they'd never paid up on.

I unbuttoned my coat and took a seat at the head of the table. "All right, gentlemen, as you know, we're here because word on the street has it that Damian Ricci is gearing up to make a move on my territory. He's been putting out feelers, gathering allies, talking to some of our suppliers, and making promises to some of those under our protection. I intend to put a stop to it before it goes any further. I've already sent someone to talk to him, but he's not a man to see reason, so this is likely to turn ugly. Needless to say, I expect your loyalty and obedience." I glanced around the table stopping when my gaze met Marco's. "Is that going to be a problem?"

"I don't like your insinuation, Marchesi."

"I don't like the fact that I don't know if I can trust you."

"My jackass of an uncle disinherited me five years ago. I ain't talked to him since. What gives you reason to doubt that?"

"I never trust anyone until they prove their loyalty to me."

Marco's expression hardened, but eventually he inclined his head toward me. "I intend to prove it."

I looked at Vinnie and Stefan next. "You've worked with the Riccis before. I need your word that you're all in with me now."

"My family and I are behind you on this," Vinnie assured me. Stefan did the same.

I looked at the two men Devil had brought in. The taller one, who I only knew as Six, responded. "Anything Muffin and I can do to send Ricci straight to hell, I want in on it."

"I need more than that. I need to know you're going to follow my orders, and that you understand if you don't, there will be consequences. Serious consequences."

"You tell me and my cousin"—he punched the other

man's shoulder—"where to go, and we'll go there, get the job done, and enjoy it. You got my word on that."

"I'm glad to be able to provide you with some entertainment."

They just smiled. I glanced at Devil, and he winked. I knew he was telling me he'd keep them in line. I trusted him to do that as much as I trusted him in anything. His loyalty was unquestionable. His ability to follow orders and agree to a plan, not so much. He'd always been a wildcard, but he was family. Over the last few years, I'd seen some of his impulsive decisions win big for us, so I'd learned to create a fuckload of contingency plans.

"Were taking this threat seriously. You wouldn't be here otherwise, but I'm not making a move now unless things escalate. So far, all I've got are a lot of rumors. I need names. I need those who were talking to the Riccis. I need the names of their wives, their girlfriends, their kids, their dogs. I want to know everything about them so when it's time to make a move, we know how to hit them where they're most vulnerable."

Angelo and Devil had wanted to make a preemptive strike, so I'd called my father to discuss my plan, and he'd given his approval. I fought the urge to smile at the memory of our conversation. I liked to make him proud. Yes, he was a hard man. Few dared to cross him, and he'd made me sorry for doing so plenty of times as a kid. But I'd always known he loved me.

When I'd come out as gay, he'd initially ranted and raved and told me how fucking inconvenient and embarrassing it was that I needed to stick my dick in some man's ass. But after one quelling look from my mother, he'd told me that while he didn't like it, nobody was going to mess with me. He'd dared anyone to say a word against me. The first man who had done so in my father's presence had gotten a bullet to the knee. After that, people kept their thoughts to themselves. That made it a hell of a lot easier for Angelo and Devil to let everyone know they were bi. I doubted Devil would've cared, but Angelo wanted our father's approval as much as I did.

"When we make a move against them, I want to keep them guessing. We'll go after their weakest allies first. I want to make Ricci sweat. We'll work from the bottom up until we have Ricci in a stranglehold. I want him stripped of everything, his money, his power, his friends. I want him on his knees, ready to beg me for mercy. He's mine. Am I clear about that?"

"Yes sir," Vinnie said.

I looked to Stefan next. "Very clear, sir."

"Are you sure they're going to move slow with this?" Marco asked. I already didn't like his lack of team spirit. I was almost hoping I found out he did still have family connections because that would give me an excuse to make sure I never had to work with him again. But I knew better than to start trouble when there was no need. Once a guy started going out looking for trouble, more of it came to him. I'd seen more than one family lose their footing because they thought they had to start a fight over everything. That's how you got yourself overextended.

"Let me repeat this for you once more and maybe this time listen and act like you got a brain cell left in your head. I'm running this show. You work for me. You do what I say. If you've got concrete intel you want to share or if you've got reason to believe your family's making a move, then I expect you to bring that to the table, but if all you've got are opinions, that's no good. The only opinion that counts here is mine."

"Yes, sir. I'll get you the intel you need." I could tell he was working hard to keep his expression neutral.

"See that you do and that no one finds out what you're up to."

"I know how to keep secrets, sir." The last word came out through gritted teeth.

"I hope to hell you do." I turned to Six and Muffin.

"We're on it, boss."

"Excellent."

"Don't they get questioned?" Marco asked, looking toward Angelo and Devil.

"Are you suggesting my brother and my cousin aren't loyal to me?"

Devil slapped his hands on the table and stood. "You don't want to go there, Marco. I don't fucking care what anybody says about me, but you talk shit about Angel, and I'll be up in your face. You got that?"

Marco held up his hands. "Fine. I just thought we should all check in."

"What did I tell you about thinking?" I asked.

"You want me to remind him, Luce?" Devil asked. I saw the spark of excitement in his eyes. It had been too long since he'd gotten himself in trouble, and he was spoiling for a fight.

I held Marco's gaze. It took a few seconds, but he dropped his eyes to the table and said, "Forgive me, sir. I don't do good with having my loyalty questioned."

"This is your last chance, Ricci."

"Yes, sir."

I surveyed all the men in the room. "Does anyone else have any questions?"

No one said anything. "Then I'm done here. I've got a client coming in soon. Angelo will give you each a set of targets and talk through the rest of the details."

I needed to meet with the contractor who was finishing up the final touches on DiGiulio's, the restaurant I was opening soon. It was the first project I'd taken on that was solely for me, and I was determined to have everything perfect. Leaving the meeting early also gave me the chance to give Angelo more responsibility. I'd always known I'd be the one who took over for our father, but I wanted Angelo to feel like our empire was his too. He needed to know I trusted him with the serious stuff.

As I walked out, I laid a hand on Devil's shoulder. He turned and glanced at me. I didn't need to say anything. I just gave him a look he knew meant that I was counting on him to keep himself in check so I didn't have to manage him while I was managing the rest of this.

He lifted his chin toward me. "You got it, boss."

I smiled at him, shaking my head as I walked out of the room.

I had more time than I'd let on before my next meeting, but I had business to attend to that I didn't want to mention to anyone yet.

"In my office," I said as I passed Carla's desk.

"So you're talking to me now?"

I didn't bother to respond to that. She closed the door to my office behind her and took a seat in front of my desk. "Are you all right?"

"I'm fine. I have some things I need you to do. This is top priority."

"First, about Peter—"

I'd known she'd want to interrogate me. "We're not talking about him."

"He's shaken, but he's doing an excellent job. I showed him the appointment calendar and how to work the phone system. Then I gave him a few things to do for me. I thought it would be better for him to be busy."

I closed my eyes and drew in a breath. I trusted Carla implicitly, but I hated that she sensed any weakness in me. "Thank you."

"One other thing. He'll need a salary offer and a contract if he's going to be a legitimate employee."

"He's working off Jimmy's debt, so make up a number and be generous with his benefits."

"How quickly do you want the debt paid off?"

I considered that. I would provide Peter with everything he needed, but I didn't want this debt hanging between us for too long. "Six months."

Carla's eyes widened. "Doesn't Jimmy owe over a hundred thousand?"

"Yes."

"Wow. He must be… skilled."

"Don't." I snarled. "He's to be treated with respect."

She started to speak, and I held up my hand. "I know I've permitted you to be frank with me, but this is something you need to keep your mouth closed about."

"Yes, sir," she snapped, making very clear how pissed off she was.

"Carla, please."

"All right. Since you said the magic word, but don't hurt that boy. I think he's actually as sweet as he seems."

I should send him away, find him a job somewhere safe and secure where I wouldn't run into him again. But I wasn't going to do that, at least not until I'd taken everything I wanted from him. I was selfish and used to getting what I wanted, and he was too fucking delectable for me to let him walk away.

"You said you had some high priority tasks for me?"

I nodded, thankful she was dropping the subject.

"Does it have to do with the meeting? It sounded like things got tense in there."

"When are they not?"

She smiled. "Never, but you don't always bring people here whose loyalty is in question."

Carla didn't like the vibe she got from Marco. I couldn't say I blamed her. The man was a sleaze. I wouldn't let him near any women under my protection. As far as I knew, he was one hundred percent straight, but if he even looked at Peter, I'd cut his eyes out. I didn't care what alliance I fucked up.

"Peter's apartment is unsafe and unsightly, and while he's working off his cousin's debt he won't be able to pay the rent. I'm moving him to my house."

She studied me for a moment, then simply said, "Yes, sir" as she typed something on her tablet. "See how I'm not making commentary?"

"You know I've shot men for less backtalk than you give me."

"They don't make your life run smoothly."

She had me there. "Things are heating up with the Ricci situation. I don't want Peter caught in the crossfire."

"Of course you don't." I didn't like the knowing look she gave me, but I let it go. "I assume you need me to arrange to have his things brought to your house."

"Yes. But more importantly, he needs new clothes, shoes, toiletries, anything else that would make him comfortable. And a room needs to be readied for him."

She frowned. "He needs a room of his own?"

"According to Virginia Woolf, yes."

She glared at me. "Cute."

"Can you manage that by the end of the day?"

"I'm insulted that you would ask that. I could have three beautiful boys of your liking outfitted and moved in by midafternoon if you required it. That's why you love me."

"Out." I pointed at the door.

"I'll take care of it, and Lucien?"

I sighed. "What?"

"Be careful with this one."

"I'll try."

## 7

## PETER

I was updating some client records Carla had asked me to assist her with when I felt Lucien's presence. I hadn't heard him approach, but the buzz across my skin told me he was there. I looked up and saw him watching me. His expression was softer than I'd ever seen it. "How may I help you, sir?"

He smiled. "You've done enough for the day. Go ahead and close out what you're doing. I have a car waiting to take you to your new home."

I stared at him. "What do you mean new home?"

"Your apartment is unsafe, impossible to secure, likely rat-infested, and in need of a long list of repairs. It's not suitable for you in any way, so as part of your employment compensation, I've made new living arrangements for you. Some of your things have been moved there already, and the rest will arrive tomorrow."

"You broke into my apartment? You had someone pack up my things? You can't just—"

He sighed. "Are we really going to go through this again? I can do anything I want."

My chest felt so tight I wasn't sure I could get enough air. "Wh-what if I don't want to move?"

"Are you telling me you're happy with your apartment, that you would choose to live there if you could afford better?"

"But I can't afford better, and you're not even going to be paying me."

"You don't need to worry about that because housing comes with the job."

I shook my head, and the room started to spin around me. "Receptionist jobs do not include housing."

"They do when they work for me."

"Did your last receptionist receive this benefit?"

He shrugged. "No, and she didn't qualify for some other benefits you're going to be getting as well."

This wasn't happening. "Please don't make me do this."

"Moving isn't optional, and this discussion is over. There's a car waiting downstairs, and I have people waiting on me. I will speak with you later tonight."

"Not tomorrow?"

"No. There are clearly more things we need to get straight between us, but this isn't the place to do that."

I glanced over at Carla who was very pointedly not looking at us. "Why are you doing this?"

"Because I've decided you're mine."

He'd sent men to force me here today. He'd spanked me in his office. Why had I thought he'd let me have any freedom? "Am I your prisoner?"

"That's such an ugly word. You're under my protection. That means I need to keep you close."

"I should never have listened to Jimmy."

"No. But I'm glad you did."

I was fighting back tears by the time I reached the lobby.

The men who'd brought me to the office that morning were waiting for me. "Mr. Kelly, your car is just outside. I'm Ralph, by the way, according to Mr. Marchesi, we'll be seeing a lot more of each other."

"Thank you." What else was there to say? I apparently belonged to Lucien now.

Was that really so bad, though? I didn't know anymore. Of course I didn't want to go home to my sad, dingy apartment where the shower dripped, the kitchen floor was warped and crumbling, and the walls were so thin I knew all my neighbors' business. I'd yet to see a rat inside my apartment, but there were plenty of roaches to keep me company. Who wouldn't want something nicer? And why shouldn't that be part of an employment package? There were jobs that came with housing.

They probably didn't require you to fuck your boss, though. I wasn't a whore. I'd never gone there, and I didn't want to do it now. I thought I was turning down Jimmy's offer of a sugar daddy, but apparently that was what I'd accepted anyway. And worse, Lucien wasn't going to let me walk away, though I was probably fooling myself to think any of the other men Jimmy would've sent me to would have let me go either, at least not without beating me half to death first. The fucked-up thing was I liked Lucien, and all my instincts told me he wasn't going to hurt me, not enough to cause lasting damage anyway. I was sure he would hurt me again in the way he had that morning, but I had liked that all too much.

As the car made slow progress through the evening traffic, I tried not to think too much more about my predicament. If I found a way out, I would take it, and until then, I'd survive like I always had and maybe even let myself enjoy it. I wondered what my new apartment would be like. I expected

Lucien to give me a decent apartment, one where I didn't feel nervous every time I came home, but as we drove through the North End, I began to wonder where he'd found something for me that wasn't outrageously overpriced. When the car slowed as we passed an idyllic row of homes, my pulse sped up. Then Ralph turned in to an actual, honest-to-God, off-the-street parking spot. I tapped on the glass that separated me from the men I assumed were Lucien's bodyguards. Ralph slid the window open, and I asked, "Where are we?"

"Marchesi's home. This is where he told us to take you."

"He has an apartment here?"

Ralph snorted. "He owns the whole building. Lives here with his family."

Fuck. Lucien hadn't gotten me a new place to live; he was moving me in with him.

A woman who looked to be in her early sixties answered the door. She had gray hair pulled into a low ponytail, and she was wearing a serviceable black dress with a white apron over it. "I'm Lola, the housekeeper. You must be Peter."

"Yes, ma'am."

"Do come in. Your room is ready, and everything Mr. Lucien ordered has been delivered and taken there for you."

"Do you mean the things from my apartment?"

"Oh, yes, those too but also all the things he purchased."

What had Lucien done? "I didn't realize he had…"

"He might have gone a little overboard. It was hard to fit everything in initially, so I had to go ahead and unpack some things and hang them up. I hope you don't mind."

"Oh, no. I don't mind at all."

"That's great, dear. Would you like a tour of the house first or would you prefer to go ahead and settle in?"

The whole situation was surreal. Lola was warm and relaxed, and she treated me like an honored guest, not a prisoner or her boss's trick. Lucien's home wasn't what I would've expected. It was clear he was extremely wealthy— he employed a housekeeper after all. But inside, it was bright with vibrant colors and plenty of light. The furnishings looked expensive but not stuffy. It was definitely not the opulent mobster house of my imagination, decorated in red and gold with lots of dark wood.

I supposed I might as well have a tour of the house since, apparently, I was going to be living there until Lucien tired of me or I found a way to escape. A tour of the house would at least show me some escape options.

*Do you really think you'd get far?*

I didn't, but I refused to think about that.

"A tour would be great. Thank you."

"Of course," Lola said. "I'll show you to the dining room first. If Lucien doesn't have other plans for you for dinner, you'll dine here at eight o'clock."

The dining room was decorated in vibrant greens and yellows. The gleaming wood table had intricately carved legs, but the matching chairs looked sturdy enough to hold Lucien and his relatives.

"Breakfast is served at seven and lunch at one, when-ever you're home for those meals. You can always request something be brought to your room or come down to the kitchen for whatever you need. I want you to feel at home here."

Captivity sounded much better than my day-to-day life: food anytime I wanted it and people to bring it to me. Maybe I should've looked into this whole being a plaything to a mobster earlier.

Lola showed me the kitchen which was done in a French country style. There was a platter of chocolate chip cookies on the counter, and she insisted I have one.

"Wow, these are delicious," I said after chewing my first bite.

"Thank you. Mr. Lucien has a bit of a sweet tooth, so I like to keep something around for him." I tried to imagine Lucien swooning over a cookie, but it was impossible.

The kitchen was so inviting I almost didn't want to leave, but I followed Lola through a sitting room, the formal living room, and then upstairs. As we reached the landing, a door opened down the hall, and Angelo stepped out.

"Ah, my brother brought you home. I'm not surprised."

"Peter will be staying with us for a while, Mr. Angelo. Your brother has asked that—"

"I be on my best behavior? When am I not?" He blew a kiss to Lola then raced down the stairs, taking them two at a time.

Lola sniffed. "That one. He's been like that since he was a child. But he's loyal to Lucien, and you can trust him. For anything."

I wondered how much she knew about the family. If she'd been with them since Angelo and Lucien were children, then she had to know a lot, probably more than she let on. "How many family members live here?"

"Four. Mr. Lucien's father, Franco Marchesi, isn't here now, though. He's spending several months in the Bahamas, but Mr. Franco's sister, Sabrina, has lived here since she left her husband, and Mr. Lucien's brother, Angelo, and their cousin Devil are part of the household. The three of them are on this floor, but I put you in the guest room next to Mr. Lucien. I assumed he'd prefer that." We continued on to the third floor.

I'd assumed Lucien would prefer me to be waiting in his bed, but I was glad I'd have my own space, not that I had any illusions he wouldn't burst in whenever he chose.

Lola opened the door and gestured for me to enter. I stared in awe. The room was much larger than the closet-like bedroom in my apartment. The color palette included varying shades of blue and white. There was a queen-sized bed with a beautifully carved pine frame. The bed itself would have filled the entire bedroom in my apartment, but here, there was room for a chaise as well as a desk matching the style of the bed. The floor was hardwood, but a pale blue rug lay under the bed, and it looked like it would feel heavenly under my feet. In front of the low-backed, cream-colored sofa lay another rug in a darker blue.

"I've placed the things from your apartment here." She pointed to some matching suitcases that were against the wall by a door I guessed led to a closet.

"That's not my luggage."

"Carla selected it for you, but if it's not to your liking, let me know."

"Oh, it's not that. It's just that I…"

"Mr. Lucien likes buying nice things. You'll get used to it."

I didn't think I would, nor would it be good for me to.

"This is your bathroom." She indicated a different door. It was twice the size of the one in my apartment. There was a tub as well as a shower. The tile, towels, and bathmat were dark blue, and the rest was bright white and so clean it sparkled.

"Is everything satisfactory?" Lola asked.

I realized I'd been gawking and not really paying attention. "It's lovely. I'm just a bit overwhelmed."

"Wait until you see the closet."

I wasn't sure I could handle that. She opened the door next to the suitcases, and as I suspected, the closet was huge —at least by city standards—and it was filled with clothes.

Not my own clothes, which would hardly have taken up a tenth of the space, but clothes so far out of my price range I was afraid to touch them. There were shoe boxes on the floor and several bags that seemed to be filled with bottles of shampoo, body wash, and who knew what other products.

"All this is for me?"

Lola smiled. "Yes. I considered taking these into the bathroom"—she gestured toward the bags filled with all manner of toiletries—"but I thought you might want to arrange them yourself."

I thought about my shower at home. The only things in there were a bar of soap and bottles of shampoo and conditioner. "I'm sure I don't need all of this."

"Mr. Lucien wants you to be comfortable here. Use whatever you need, and if there's anything else you'd like, just let me know."

Would he really buy anything for me? "I can't accept all this."

"You'll have to discuss that with Mr. Lucien."

I could imagine how that conversation would go. Lucien did whatever he wanted, and I was expected to accept it. I got up the nerve to reach out and touch one of the shirts. The fabric was so soft and would feel amazing sliding against my skin. I should refuse all of this and try to figure out how to convince Lucien to let me go, but I couldn't help but fantasize about how wonderful it would be to be his pampered princess. What would he expect of me in return?

More than I was willing to give? Maybe not. I definitely didn't mind working as a receptionist, and I'd been given far less work to do than in the offices where I'd temped. I was still a little afraid of Carla, but she never demeaned me or expected too much, and she was incredibly competent, which was more than I could say for most of the people I'd worked with.

"Do you have any other questions?" Lola asked.

I had so many questions, but none of them were for Lola, and most of them would likely go unanswered. "No. Thank you."

"I'll leave you here then. As I said before, dinner is at eight. I'm sure Mr. Lucien will let you know if he has other plans once he arrives." Before she reached the door, she turned back. "I almost forgot. There's a phone for you on the nightstand. Mr. Lucien will contact you on it if he has a message for you."

"I already have a phone."

She smiled. "Mr. Lucien would like you to use that one. The number is written on the box, and his number is already programmed in."

"Thank you." What else was there for me to say?

"You're welcome. Please don't hesitate to ask if there's anything else you need." She left then.

I crossed the room on wobbly legs and flopped down on the sofa. I looked around the room once more. The closet door stood open, and I wondered how many thousands of dollars the collection of clothes and shoes represented. More than I made last year probably.

What would happen if I tried to leave? Was Ralph waiting outside to make sure I stayed put? What would happen if I left and Lucien didn't send someone to bring me back? I'd go back to searching for temp jobs and living in my shitty apartment that would seem even worse after being tempted with this beautiful room. I'd also go back to dreaming of a man who'd treat me like I meant something, a strong man who could protect me and take care of me so I could stop worrying about survival for just a little while. A man just like Lucien.

He was the man I'd been dreaming of in almost every way, but in my fantasies, my prince was never a criminal.

A little while later, Lucien messaged me. He said that some unexpected business was taking him out of town for the night, and he would see me the next day. Not wanting to eat dinner with Lucien's family, I found Lola in the kitchen and asked if I could take something up to my room. She prepared a tray for me and brought me another the next morning for breakfast. Ralph drove me to work, and Carla made sure I knew what my duties were for the day.

Lucien never showed up at the office, and when it was time for me to leave, Ralph was once again waiting for me in the lobby. The longer I existed in the strange new world without Lucien there to anchor me, the more agitated I felt. I needed some piece of normality, some reminder of who I really was. As Ralph held open the car door for me, I said, "I'd like to go see my uncle."

He shook his head. "My orders are to take you back to the boss's house."

"Are you saying I'm not allowed to go anywhere but the house or this office?"

He shrugged. "Those are my orders."

"Where is Lucien?"

"It's not my business to ask questions. I just do what I'm told."

"Please take me to my uncle's bar. I just want to talk to him. You can stay and make sure I don't leave."

Ralph shook his head. "You can call your uncle. The boss won't mind that, but I can't take you anywhere except home."

"It's not my home."

"As you say."

Angry as I was, I couldn't blame Ralph for not wanting to cross Lucien. I'd been following his orders too. The extent to which my life was under Lucien's control hadn't really hit me before, not even when I'd spent the night in his house. It had all still seemed like a dream, but now, knowing Lucien was controlling all my movements, panic set in. My heart raced, and my chest felt tight. I needed to see Lucien, to talk to him, to explain that I couldn't belong to him. I needed to know if he would listen to me or if I was truly a prisoner.

I struggled to keep from having a breakdown on the ride to Lucien's house. As soon as we arrived, I rushed upstairs to my room. I didn't even reach the bed before I crumpled into a heap and let the tears come.

## 8

---

## LUCIEN

After meeting with my new buyer, it came to my attention that there was an issue with a chop shop in New Jersey that we had an understanding with. The automotive division of our criminal enterprises dealt solely in high-end car parts, but these fuckers were trying to mix in low-end shit and charge top prices. I decided the situation needed some personal attention.

I hadn't liked leaving Peter alone on his first night at my house, but I also hadn't wanted him to see the side of me that was going to come out when I confronted the men who thought they could double-cross me. I'd known there would be blood, a lot of it, and Peter seemed like the kind of guy that might not do well with that. Also, what was the point of trying to protect him if I brought him into a confrontation. He was better off in Lola's care. I just hoped Angelo and Devil hadn't given him any shit. After the day I'd had, they'd be fucking sorry if I found out they'd shown him any disrespect.

Lola came to greet me when I entered the house. As she took my coat, she said, "You look exhausted, Mr. Lucien. Can I get something for you?"

I wanted bourbon, but I wanted to see Peter more. "Have a bottle of my best bourbon and two glasses sent to Peter's room."

She nodded. "Yes, sir."

I could tell she wanted to say something else. "What is it Lola? Is Peter all right?"

"He seemed upset when he came in a little while ago."

"Thank you. I'll check on him." I hurried upstairs to Peter's room, glad for once that Angelo and Devil were rarely home this time of day. I would brief them in the morning about what happened during my trip to New Jersey.

I didn't bother knocking. When I stepped into Peter's room, he was lying on the rug by the bed in a crumpled heap.

"Peter?" I sank down beside him. "What's wrong?"

He turned to look at me, and I saw that his eyes were red and his cheeks tear stained.

"You wouldn't let me... I can't go see my uncle... You have me trapped here, and I... I can't do this."

"What do you mean I wouldn't let you see your uncle?"

"I asked to go to his bar after work, and Ralph said he had to bring me here, that his orders were to only take me to the office or back here, so..."

Fuck. I had told Ralph that but not because I intended to prevent Peter from going anywhere else. I wanted to make sure Peter was safe and prevent him from running if he was upset about my insistence he move in with me. Sooner or later, Ricci would find out I'd staked my claim on Peter, and my beautiful boy would become a target.

When I laid a hand on Peter's back, he flinched and pulled away.

"I'm not going to hurt you."

"I know, but I can't think when you touch me."

I couldn't say I minded having that effect on him. "I did give Ralph those orders, but I'm not going to keep you from seeing your uncle. All you have to do is ask me if you want to go somewhere. I'll let Ralph know he can take you there tomorrow after work."

"I can see Uncle Mac alone?"

"Ralph will accompany you into the bar."

"How did— Never mind. Of course you know my uncle runs a bar."

I knew a hell of a lot more about him than that. "I wouldn't bring someone into my home or my business without learning everything I could about them and their family."

"Is there anything you can't learn about a person?"

I wasn't sure if he actually wanted an answer, but I gave him one anyway. "I have to get to know someone to learn how they think, who they really are, and what's in here. I laid my hand over his heart. A lot of people think most people in my world don't have a fucking heart. They're wrong. Most of them don't ever show it, though, so you have to look closely."

Peter studied me as if taking my words to heart. "I want to know who you really are."

"It's probably best that you don't."

Peter shook his head. "You're more than a cold, hard man who expects to get everything he wants."

"I'm everything my upbringing has made me. I'm a criminal who's seen and done horrible things, but I was lucky enough to have parents who truly loved me. My mother"—I paused to cross myself—"God rest her soul, wanted to teach me how to care, not just how to kill, and my father defended me to anyone who thought to dismiss me because I'm gay."

"If you know how to be a good man, then why have you taken my freedom from me?"

I refused to let him see how much his words hurt. Did he really see me as a monster? "I have a lot of enemies, Peter. It's not safe for you to be out without protection."

"Is it really about protecting me, or do you just want to make sure you don't lose your property?"

"That's not how I see you, Peter." I hated the pain I saw in his eyes.

"You said you owned me, and you won't let me leave."

I had said those exact words, and I meant them, but not the way he was taking them. "I want you, and that means you're under my protection."

"And you always get what you want."

"I do, but I want to give you what you want too." More than anything, I wanted to give him pleasure.

"Is this what you think I want? This beautiful room and all these clothes? Jesus, it must've cost a fortune, and I've never owned so many hair and skin products in my life."

I let my gaze slide over his beautiful face. "You don't need them."

"Why did you buy them for me then?"

"I told Carla to make sure your room was fully stocked. If there was anything you needed or wanted, it should be here for you."

"What if what I want is to leave?"

I held his gaze. "Is it? Really?"

"I can't deny that I'm attracted to you. There'd be no point after yesterday. But you can't just… You can't pay me off with all these things. You've already proven I'll obey you. Haven't you humiliated me enough without trying to pay me off. I'm not your whore, Lucien."

Molten anger boiled through me. "How dare you—"

His eyes widened, and he scooted away from me. I made myself take a deep breath. When I'd seen him looking so devastated, I'd wanted to comfort him. I didn't want him sad or frightened, but how dare he take what was supposed to be a gift and…

*He doesn't understand your world.*

"Only the work you do at the office goes to pay off Jimmy's debt. The clothes and everything else are gifts. I wanted to show you how good you will have it with me."

"It's too much. This is all too much. I never meant to—"

"But you did. You walked into my world, and it hasn't all been bad has it? Remember how it felt when I reddened your ass, the way you whimpered, the way you were so hard you nearly came before I touched you."

"I didn't."

I raised my brows. "You've insulted me, and now you're lying to me. I won't have that, Peter."

"I enjoyed it, but that doesn't mean…"

"That you want me? Yes, it does."

"Lucien, I'm not…"

"Not what?"

"A plaything or property."

"You're a man who craves dominance and control. You long for someone to tell you what to do and then expect you to do it." His chest rose and fell rapidly, and his eyes were huge. He watched me like a rabbit would watch a fox. I was going to claim my scared little rabbit, but while he might be prey, he would enjoy being eaten, and he would thrive under my care.

I moved closer so I could stroke the fluttering pulse at his neck. He stiffened, but he didn't try to pull away. "You're scared, but you're also turned on. I see it in your eyes." I trailed my other hand down his chest. He sucked in his breath, and I continued the caress, over his flat belly and along his inner thigh. His pulse beat even faster now. I curled my hand around his neck as I pressed the heel of my other palm to his hard dick. "I'm right, aren't I? I see you. I know what you need."

Peter's tongue slid over his lips, leaving them wet. "I… I don't…"

"Don't lie to me, Peter. Lies will be punished."

"The truth scares me."

It scared me too, but I couldn't tell him that. He needed to see my strength, not my weaknesses. I brushed my lips against the side of his face and blew warm breath into his ear, making him shudder. How certain was I of his true feelings? I took risks all the time, but this felt different even than those that meant life or death.

I always faced my fears, though, so I pulled him to me and spoke against his ear. "I'm giving you a choice right now. You can go back to the life you were leading. I'll have someone watch over you until I'm sure you haven't drawn the interest of my enemies, but you won't see me again. Or you can stay. Be mine. Let me protect you and care for you. You'll want for nothing."

He turned to look at me. Desire still burned in his eyes, but I could also see fear. "What will you expect of me?"

"Obedience. I need to be in control. I can't change who I am." I released him and waited for his response.

He closed his eyes for several seconds, and I held my breath. Then he looked at me like he could see deeper into me than I'd let anyone. "I'm not a risk taker. I'm not someone who seeks out danger. I know this is crazy. I know I don't belong here. I want to stay with you, but when trouble comes, I always run."

"What if I made sure you couldn't?"

I pushed his knees apart and forced him to lie back as I moved over him, taking his hands and dragging them along the carpet until I had them pinned over his head.

"You're not making it easy to think."

I tilted my hips, dragging my hard cock over his. "Maybe I don't want you to think. Maybe I only want you to feel."

He arched up, working himself against me, and I knew then that I had him as surely as when he'd knelt for me.

"You deserve so much more than you've had. I can give that to you."

"And take… what?"

I thrust against him harder. "Everything."

He groaned. "How do you make that sound so good?"

"I've spent my life learning how to make people do what I want."

"I should fight this, fight you."

"No." I moved my hips slowly, sliding against him and making him moan. "I'm the best thing that's ever happened to you."

"You're dangerous."

"I am. And I'm ruthless and arrogant. But you need a man like me."

"I don't want to need you."

I tightened my grip on his wrists and thrust against him harder. "But you do."

"I… Yes."

I let him go and sat back on my heels. "Stay or go? Tell me your choice."

"I thought…"

"I need to hear it clearly."

A few seconds passed as he stared at me, his hazel eyes full of heat and need. I should've been ashamed of myself for seducing him until he didn't really have a choice, but

I'd made him an offer, and that was more than I wanted to do.

"I'll stay."

"Good choice. Now come here." I leaned back against the bed and gestured to the spot on the floor between my legs. He moved, slowly, cautiously, crawling toward me. Fuck, he was a beautiful sight. "That's it." I laid my hands on his shoulders and pushed gently. "Turn around and lean against me."

He did, and for a moment, I simply enjoyed the heat of him. "Relax," I whispered against the side of his head.

It took a little while, but eventually, he sank back and let me take his weight.

"Perfect." I slid my hands down his chest to the fastenings of his pants. He tensed again when I undid the button and began to lower his zipper. "Remember what you agreed to. You're mine."

I expected a protest, but he melted into me again. Fuck, his submissive side was too good. I pulled out his cock and stroked it slowly. I wasn't going to rush this. In fact, a little edging was a fitting punishment for not being honest with me.

"I'm going to have you tonight." I gripped him just a little tighter and was rewarded with a sharp intake of breath. "You're going to enjoy it, but I'm going to take it slow, ramp you up until you're begging, until you can't wait a second longer."

He bit his lip, muffling his whimper.

"No. You're not allowed to hide anything from me. I want it all, remember? All the sounds you make." I slid my hand over his cockhead on my upstroke. "Every inch of this gorgeous body. All your need. You'll give that to me. Do you understand?"

"What happens if I get scared and try to run from you?"

I remembered how good he looked with my handprints on his red ass. "You know what will happen."

"You'll spank me. Maybe c-cane me."

"Jesus, I love the catch in your voice when you say that. The way you shiver. You can ask for it if you need it, you know? The discipline. The pain."

"And if I do something worse than that?"

"Worse than leaving me?"

"You said I could leave if I wanted to."

"I gave you a choice. You chose to stay. Now you are utterly mine."

"I... I know what you do to your enemies, and—"

I grabbed his shoulder and jerked him around to face me. "What did I promise you?"

"That you would protect me and keep me safe."

"That's right, so answer your own question."

"You're really going to take care of me?"

"I don't make promises I don't intend to keep." He was still wary of me and worried I'd hurt him, but he'd chosen to stay. His instincts were telling him he needed my dominance. I needed to figure out how to get him to believe those instincts.

I repositioned him like he'd been before and started working his cock again. "I am going to punish you tonight."

"Wh-why? Because I questioned you?"

"Do you think I should punish you for that?"

"I don't know."

That was certainly something to consider for the future. He was going to be so much fun. "I'm punishing you because I expect complete honesty from you, and you tried to lie to me."

"I was scared."

"Your punishment will help settle you, and eventually you'll learn to trust what I say, to know I'm protecting you."

He turned his head to look at me. Then his gaze dropped to my waist. "Are you going to use your belt on me?"

I smiled, loving the way he'd revealed he was eager for that. "Not tonight. Tonight, I have something else in mind."

## 9

## PETER

L ucien's hand on my cock felt so fucking good. He was moving faster now, pausing occasionally to tease my slit and rub his thumb along the frenulum. I couldn't stop watching his hand as he played with me. I was a mouse trusting a cat to do right by me. He'd given me a chance to run, and I should have taken it. Instead, I was ignoring the responsible side of my brain that had helped me to survive and falling right into the arms of denial.

I whimpered when he squeezed me particularly tight. Heat rose in my cheeks, but I knew he wanted the sounds, so I gave them to him. I wanted his control.

Pleasure heated me until my balls were high and tight. I was going to come soon. I whined and squirmed in his arms, lifting my hips, trying to drive my cock into the circle of his fingers. I wanted to watch myself come. I wanted to see it soak his hand and run down over his fingers.

"Please, Lucien. Please don't stop. I'm so—"

He kept going, hand moving faster. I was right there, I could feel the buzz in my balls, the tension in my muscles. He let go, and I gasped. "No. I was so close."

"I know you were," he said nuzzling my neck. "But I'm not ready for you to come yet. I'm going to teach you a lesson by making you wait. I'm going to tease you until you start to wonder if it will actually be a relief to come or just more pain."

"Lucien, please."

He growled. "Do you know how much I love it when you say my name in that breathless voice? I want to hear you cry it out as I drive inside you."

He'd nearly wrecked me the day before with nothing but his hand. What would it be like to feel him buried in me? I needed to find out. Now. "Please. I want to give you that."

His laugh sent a shiver through me. "Don't worry. We'll get there, but you have to take your punishment first."

The immediate urgency to come had receded, but my cock ached, and I was still as hard as ever.

"Take off your clothes and lie on your back on the bed." I nearly fell as I tried to stand on my shaky legs. Lucien rose gracefully from the floor and took my arm. "You can always ask for my help if you need it."

"I'm a little dizzy."

Lucien pushed my pants down for me. He removed my shoes and socks and helped me climb onto the bed, joining me and kneeling between my legs as he unbuttoned my shirt. When he had me completely naked, he arranged some pillows for me to lie back on.

"Watch me," he commanded. Still fully dressed himself, he took hold of my ankles, encouraging me to bring my feet up and place them flat on the mattress. His fingers skimmed along my perineum, then he teased my balls as his gaze swept the length of me. "You're as beautiful as I knew you would be."

"I—" He reached up and placed a finger against my lips.

"Never contradict a compliment I give you. I know what I see, a gorgeous man who needs someone to teach him all about pleasure."

"Yes, please."

He smiled and then shocked the hell out of me by lowering his head and licking the length of my cock. My shaft jumped against his tongue. He looked up, and our gazes met. He continued to watch me watch him as he teased my head, circling it with his tongue. I couldn't breathe. I was too stunned. I hadn't thought that he would use his mouth on me like that.

He continued to hold my gaze as he swallowed more and more, taking nearly all of me before sliding his lips back up along the length. He lapped at the precum beaded at my slit. "Fuck, you taste so good, Peter. I want more."

He took me deep in his throat again, sucking, teasing, and working me. Just the knowledge that he would do this was enough to have me desperate as fuck to come. And the way he made me feel, his hot mouth, the clasp of his throat as he swallowed around me… I'd never had any man's mouth that even compared to this. I fought the desire to lift my hips and push deeper into him, but I knew he needed to keep control, and I wanted it that way.

He slipped a hand between my legs, circling my hole. Suddenly, I was right there on the edge, ready to tip over. "Lucien, I—"

He pulled off, and I struggled to draw in air as I looked up at him. His lips were red and shiny with spit, and his eyes were dark. "I know how to pleasure a man, Peter."

"I just never thought you'd do that. Fuck, you're so hot." I felt the heat in my face and knew I was blushing, but at least it distracted me from the ache in my balls. How many more times would he bring me to the edge without letting me come? I already knew my climax was going to hurt as much as it felt good.

Lucien sat back on his heels, and his gaze raked over me. "There are a lot of things you don't know about me, both good and bad. Some of them are things I'll never be able to tell you. Some I hope you'll forgive me for, and some I know you're going to love." He lifted one of my feet and began massaging it, digging his fingers into my arch and making me groan just like his mouth on my cock had. "That feels incredible."

"Relax and enjoy it." He thoroughly loosened up every muscle in my right foot. Then he took the left into his hands and did the same thing.

"Look at me, Peter."

I'd watched him at first when he began to massage my feet, but seeing the tender expression on his face as he concentrated solely on giving me pleasure had been too much for me. I didn't need to get my hopes up that there might be something more between us. That would only lead to trouble and heartbreak. Lucien would eventually tire of me and let me go. I believed he would protect me and wouldn't hurt me physically, but he could destroy my heart if I let myself fall for him.

I couldn't pretend he was the prince I'd longed for. I would enjoy this while it lasted. It wasn't like I wanted to be involved with a man like him long term anyway. I didn't want to constantly be in danger. I was tempted to think I was brave for not running from him when I had the chance, but that wasn't true. I'd still taken the path of least resistance. And I had no intention of involving myself in Lucien's criminal activities. I belonged in the background, not in the spotlight, certainly not on the arm of a man like Lucien Marchesi.

I sucked in my breath when I met his gaze. He looked

predatory once again, the way he had the first time he'd taken me into his office and made me kneel for him. I'd done it, and I knew I would do it again. I would do whatever he asked, but I had to keep my heart out of it.

"Stroke yourself, Peter. I'm going to watch, and you're going to watch me watch. I want to see the need in your eyes and the agony when I deny you again."

He'd thoroughly relaxed me with the foot massage, but now my heart was racing again, my breathing shallow. How did he manage that with nothing but a few words?

"Peter." The command in his voice made me shiver. I reached for my cock, wrapping my hand around it. I stroked myself slowly at first and then faster as my body demanded more. Lucien smiled as he watched me, and his eyes darkened.

"That's it. Show me how you bring yourself off. Show me how you make yourself come."

His hand was pressed against his own cock, rubbing himself through his pants. Seeing how turned on he was from watching me made me long to please him even more. I knew he would order me to stop soon, and the closer I brought myself to coming, the harder that would be. But I couldn't slow my strokes, not with him watching me like he wanted to devour me. I kept dropping my gaze to his hand on his cock and then looking into his eyes again, seeing his need. "Lucien, please, I—"

"Don't stop yet," he ordered. I didn't. I worked myself until I didn't think I could hold back anymore. What would he do if I came without his permission?

"Tease your balls with your other hand."

Oh God. "Please, I can't."

"You can because I want you to."

He was so fucking arrogant. Why was that such a turn on?

I cupped my balls and tugged on them, pushing myself to the very edge. Lucien held my gaze. I couldn't have looked away, not for anything. When I was absolutely sure I'd pushed myself too far, he pulled me back. "Stop. Put your hands at your sides."

I pressed my hands into the mattress and held utterly still. I was afraid even a current of air could make my cock go off.

"You're such a good boy, Peter. I love how you obey me." I tried to speak, but my mouth was too dry. "Just breathe. Slowly." He leaned forward and laid a hand against my chest. "Make my hand rise. Just focus on that."

He was watching me again. I licked my lips as I looked into his eyes. I wanted this. I wanted his control. I wanted… things I knew I couldn't have. "Lucien, I…"

He pressed a finger to my lips. "Close your eyes, baby. This is about feeling, not talking."

I lay there, trying to focus on breathing, feeling his hand on me and the mattress beneath me. My body ached with the need to come. He hadn't even touched my hole, but I felt empty inside, desperate to be filled by him.

A few moments later, he pulled his hand away, and my eyes fluttered open. I watched as he slowly undressed. All the tension and need I'd felt returned as I watched him reveal his gorgeous body. I sucked in my breath when his dress shirt dropped from his shoulders. His chest and arms were perfection. I wanted to run my hands over every ridge of muscle.

He let his fingers trail over his abs. "Impressed?"

"Yes, sir." My gaze slid over him again. "I… um… I like all of you."

"You haven't seen all of me yet."

He undid his pants. When he pushed them and his briefs over his hips, my mouth fell open. His cock was thick and as perfectly formed as the rest of him. I didn't think I'd ever thought of a man's cock as beautiful before, but Lucien's sure as hell was. He kicked out of his shoes and his pants, then took a step closer to the bed. "What do you think now that you've seen the whole package?"

"You have to know how incredible you look."

"I know what other people think, but I want to know your opinion."

Did that actually matter to him? He seemed so sure of himself. He'd known I would obey him, and I was sure he could have almost any man he wanted. But in case it truly would make a difference to him, I gave him the whole truth.

"You're the most gorgeous man I've ever seen, naked or clothed. You had my attention the second you stepped off the elevator on my first day at your office. You scared the fuck out of me, but I still wanted you. I'm still scared, but I'm here, willing to do whatever you say."

"Thank you for being honest."

I supposed it was hard to get an honest answer when you held the power Lucien did. Most men he was around probably told him whatever they thought he wanted to hear. I wondered if that was hard for him, but dwelling on his vulnerabilities would only put my heart at risk. It was easier to imagine him as all-powerful and invincible. This was supposed to be all about pleasure. "Are you going to fuck me now?"

# 10

## LUCIEN

"Hmmm." I tilted my head to the side, pretending to think. "Should I? Or should I make you suffer more?" I prowled along the side of the bed as I spoke. Peter's gaze followed me, and his breaths came faster. "I love watching you get so worked up, but I also want to drive into you, feel your ass clench around me, fuck you hard. I want you to know just how good you're going to have it if you obey me."

Peter watched me warily. There was a touch of fear in his eyes, but mostly his gaze was filled with lust and appreciation. My reaction to him telling me I was the most beautiful man he'd ever seen had startled me. I knew I looked good. I worked hard at it and paid a lot of money for it, but that sincere praise from him had sent warmth all through me. Peter wanted me, even with all the darkness I held inside. I was sure he deserved a man who was nicer than I'd ever be, one who wouldn't put him in constant danger, but he was here, his cock leaking onto his belly, ready to do whatever I said.

"Pull your legs up onto your chest, Peter. I want to see

your tight little hole. I want you as exposed to me as you can get."

"Yes, sir." My dick jumped at those soft words which seemed to fall unconsciously from his lips. What was it about this boy that affected me so much? His innocence? The way he relaxed when he gave in and obeyed? I'd had plenty of submissive men before, but there was something special about Peter's surrender. I reached into the nightstand drawer and pulled out lube and a condom.

Peter's eyes widened. "Those aren't mine."

"I gave an order that your room be fully stocked."

His cheeks were already beautifully flushed, but they turned even redder.

"Everyone—the staff, my family—knows you're here because you're mine."

"That's… um…"

"Let's focus on something else." I squirted lube onto my fingers as he watched.

"Are you going to tease me again?"

The way his voice shook made me want to, but I couldn't wait much longer to have him. My cock was demanding I end this game. I slid my finger along his crack and teased his hole. "What do you think, Peter? Are you ready to have me inside you?"

"I don't know, sir. I don't know if I'm ready for any of this."

"You're way too innocent to be here with me, but I'm not letting you go." I pushed a finger into him and groaned as his hot passage clamped down on the digit. "You're so tight, baby."

"It's been a long time, and I'm not… I don't have a lot of experience."

Holy fuck, he wasn't a virgin, was he? "You have done this before, right?"

He nodded. "Yeah, a few times, but it's never been…"

I smiled down at him as I slid my finger slowly in and out, then took his cock in my other hand and began working it with the same rhythm. "It's never been what?"

"This good. I've never… I've always been kind of disappointed."

The men he'd been with clearly did not deserve him. "I won't disappoint you. I may demand a lot of you, but you will enjoy every minute you spend in my bed. Do you understand?"

"Yes, sir. I wouldn't have stayed… if I didn't think you… if I didn't think it would be better with you."

"It will be so much better, but first, I think I need to torment you one more time."

His eyes widened, and he started to say something, but I added a second finger, and he bit down on his lower lip. I opened him up, working my fingers deeper until I was massaging his prostate. He arched off the bed and writhed as he tried to take more. He was so close. The color in his cheeks spread down his neck and over his chest, and he seemed to barely be able to breathe.

"Please, Lucien. Please."

I loved when he used my name. I worked him faster, loving that his body knew what it wanted. He might not have known how much he craved a man's control before he met me, but his body knew. He responded to me perfectly.

When I was sure he was ready to spill, I pulled my fingers from his body and let go of his cock.

"No. No, please." His eyes shone with unshed tears. His cock was red, his balls so high and tight.

"You're so responsive. So beautiful all needy like this. What if I made you wait until tomorrow to come?"

"No, you can't. You said—"

I leaned over him and pinned his wrists to the bed. "Yes, I can. I can do anything I want to you. You need to remember who's in charge. I could tie you up so there was no way you could touch yourself and leave you here, aching, needing. I could keep bringing you close to the edge all night."

"Oh God, please don't."

His distress did me in. "Don't worry. I meant it when I said I was going to have you tonight. I'm not going to walk away now."

Peter exhaled sharply. "Thank you. I'll be good. I'll do whatever you say."

I stroked his cheek. "I know you will, Peter. You want to please me."

"I do. I swear."

"Good. Right now, what would please me is your lips wrapped around my cock."

Peter whimpered as I moved up his body and straddled his shoulders. "I know you want me inside you, and you'll get that, but I've been waiting for this ever since I made you kneel in my office. The way you looked up at me, expecting me to feed you my cock had me so hard it was all I could do to hold myself back."

"Why did you?"

"I wanted to take my time with you, and my intention that day was to prove a point. You did exactly what I wanted, and making you wait made you want me more. Now open up."

I teased his lips with the tip of my cock, and he did as I said. "Eyes on me," I ordered as I made slow, shallow strokes into his mouth. He stared up at me, wonder and desire in his gaze. He was fucking perfect.

"You're so beautiful like this. One day soon I'm going to put you on your knees and fuck your face until I come down your throat, but right now, I needed you to get my cock ready to drive into your tight ass, and you needed something to distract you from the ache in your balls."

Peter moaned around me, and I wondered just how fast he could bring me off. I was close to my breaking point after waiting as long as I had for him. A few moments later, I pulled back and brushed his sweaty hair from his forehead.

"You've taken your punishment well, Peter. Now it's time to be rewarded." I settled back between his legs. I wanted to push right into him and feel his heat around my bare cock, but that wasn't something I was going to force him into, so I rolled on the condom and slicked myself up.

"I'll go slow as you adjust to me, but I'm going to fill you all the way up, take you, own you, and when I'm ready for it, you're finally going to get to come."

"Please, sir."

"Turn over." He did, wrapping his arms around the pillow, arching his back to push his needy little ass toward me. I lined up my cock at his entrance, and he gasped as I surged forward.

"You can take it. You were made to be mine." I reached underneath him and took hold of his cock. He relaxed as I worked his length, and I pushed in deeper.

"S-so big."

I chuckled. "I am, but you're ready for me. I want to be all the way inside you, and I get what I want."

Peter drove back, trying to take me deeper, so I tightened my hold on his hips. "I'm controlling this."

"Please."

I didn't know if he was asking for more or asking me to

let go. I doubted he knew either, but I eased further inside, pulled back, then gave him all of me.

"Fuck," he cried. "It burns."

I kissed the back of his neck. "You're a good boy, taking all my cock. I'm going to fuck you now, and you're going to love it."

He squirmed, trying to flex his hips as I gave him several long, slow thrusts. Then I let go so he could move like he wanted to. I didn't hold back either. I slammed into him, and he worked his hips to meet every stroke.

"Please, Lucien. Need to come. Please."

I took hold of his hips again, angling him so I'd be better able to drag across his sweet spot on every stroke. He keened when I hit him just right, and I reached for his cock again. "Who do you belong to?"

"You, Lucien. You."

"That's right. Now come for me." I stroked his cock as hard and fast as I was fucking him. "Show me how much you need this."

"Lucien!" he arched his back deeply. His ass squeezed my cock so hard it hurt as he drove himself through the circle of my fingers and came. I meant to keep going, to see if I could push him to come a second time, but as his beautiful body writhed under me and his inner muscles milked my cock, I couldn't hold back.

"Mine, Peter. You're mine," I roared as I let go and came, buried deep inside him.

Peter's legs slid out from under him, and we collapsed to the mattress. I wanted to simply fall asleep there with him, but we both needed dinner first. I kissed the back of his neck and pulled out, making him wince.

"Are you all right?" I asked.

"Yeah, but… wow. I'm going to feel that tomorrow."

"And that means you'll be thinking of me all day, just like I want you too."

He made a contented sound that had my cock trying to perk up again. "Are you hungry?"

"Mmmhmm."

Jesus, he was blissed out. I fucking loved it. "I'll get us some dinner."

I rose from the bed, discarded the condom in the bathroom trash, and opened the closet door. Peter rolled over and looked at me. "What are you doing?"

I grabbed the navy silk robe that hung on a peg just inside the door. It was tight across the shoulders, since it had been purchased for Peter, but it reached around me enough to make me semi-decent. That was all I cared about. Rather than answer him, I scooped Peter up in my arms. He made an adorable surprised squawk.

"We're going to my room. I want you with me tonight."

"What about dinner?"

"I'll have Lola bring it to us there."

"But I'm naked. What if someone sees us?"

He clung to my neck as I grabbed a blanket from the bench at the end of the bed and tossed it over him. "There. You're decent now."

When we'd finished with dinner, I noticed Peter watching me, curiosity in his eyes. "Go ahead and ask your question. I won't promise to answer, but you can ask me anything."

Peter's cheeks turned a beautiful shade of pink. "I don't even know where to begin. I want to know more about you, about your family, about what you actually do."

"Most of what I do would scare the fuck out of you— even if it wasn't dangerous to let you know too much—but I do have one project I can tell you about."

"What is it?" His eager expression made me want him again, but there would be time for that later.

"Come sit on my lap, and I'll tell you."

He slid across the sofa, and I pulled him into my arms. I couldn't remember a time when I'd felt happier than I did, curled up with Peter, telling him all about my plans for DiGiulios, the food, the décor, the ambiance I was hoping to achieve. All my dreams for the place that would be mine, not my father's, not a front for crime, just a fucking amazing restaurant.

## 11

## PETER

I never expected Lucien to want me in his bed all night. I'd assumed that once he was done fucking me, he'd expect me to sleep in my own room. But not only had he wanted me with him, he'd held me and just talked to me, telling me about his restaurant. I could hear the excitement in his voice as he described it. He didn't sound like a cold, hard, mobster; he sounded like a man filled with passion. When I'd started to doze, he'd carried me to bed and held me against him as I'd fallen asleep. Despite the numerous times my brain tried to remind me how much danger I was in and how crazy I was to have chosen to stay, I slept more soundly in Lucien's arms than I had in a long time.

His room was even larger than mine, and he had a balcony. He'd told me he loved to eat out there, but it was far too chilly for us to do so the previous night. We'd talked and laughed, and I'd felt at ease with him. When he was relaxed, it was easy to forget how scary he could be in his office. I stopped thinking about all the things he'd done and the illegal businesses he was involved in. He was just a gorgeous man sharing stories about his childhood.

When Lucien's alarm went off in the morning, it woke me with a start. I felt like I'd only been asleep for a few hours, and honestly it hadn't been much longer than that. Lucien and I had spent longer talking than we should have, and it was very late when we went to bed. Lucien shut the alarm off and stood, seeming to go from sound asleep to awake in seconds.

"Couldn't we snooze that?" I asked.

He just laughed. "I'll get in the shower first. You stay there until I'm done."

What felt like only seconds later, Lucien shook my shoulder. "Come on, sleepyhead. It's your turn in the shower. I've got a hell of a day ahead of me, and I can't be late."

I bit back the response that since he was my boss, he could give me permission to be late and dragged myself from the bed. When I stepped out of the shower, Lucien was standing at the long bathroom counter shaving. I wrapped a towel around my waist, leaned against the counter, and used my hands to hoist myself up so I could sit and watch him. His gaze met mine. "What's so interesting?"

"You. I'd enjoy watching you do just about anything." I reached out and touched his cheek. "You missed a spot."

He held his razor out to me. I took it and scooted closer to him. I held his chin with one hand, wanting to be sure he stayed still, then I very carefully slid the razor down his cheek, scraping away the shaving cream and leaving behind smooth skin. His hand wrapped around my wrist. I looked up and saw intense heat in his eyes, but there was something else there too, something softer that made my heart flutter.

"Thank you."

"You're welcome." My voice trembled, and I held out the razor to him. He took it from me and rinsed it in the sink.

"Sometimes I wonder if there's any point to this. I'll need to shave again by lunchtime."

I smiled. "I wouldn't mind you all scruffy."

"I had a feeling you wouldn't."

A few moments later, I was dressed in a blue shirt and gray dress pants which Lucien had picked out for me while I showered. I was almost ready, but I couldn't get my tie right. I was tying it for probably the fifth time when Lucien stepped up behind me, his body close but not quite touching me.

Seeing him in the mirror and feeling his warmth sent need zinging through me. I wanted him to fuck me again and then stay here with me all day. He'd be different at the office, harder, and I wanted him to stay like he'd been the night before. He reached around me and captured my wrists, pulling my hands down to my sides. "Let me."

He pressed himself fully against me as he reached for the ends of my tie. The way he held me felt as intimate as everything we'd done the night before. I held my breath as he effortlessly tied a perfect knot. "That's better."

I nodded mutely as I watched him in the mirror. The look on his face wasn't predatory at all now. It was tender and... caring? I shouldn't let myself think that way, but as he leaned into me and slid his lips over my temple and down along the line of my jaw, I shivered. My cock began to swell as I imagined him doing what I'd longed for last night but hadn't gotten, kissing on the lips. I'd dreamed about Lucien's mouth on mine since the first time I'd seen him.

"Come on. I told you we can't be late today."

His voice jolted me from my thoughts. "Oh, right. Sorry, sir."

"You're way too fucking tempting. I don't know how I'm going to get any work done with you there."

"I can always go back to—"

"The fuck you can." His arms tightened around me. "You aren't leaving. You made a choice."

"I just meant that I don't have to work in your office."

"Yes, you do. I made a promise to protect you. Keeping you with me is part of it."

"Okay." He took my hand and tugged me along behind him. "I need my bag, and wh-what about breakfast?"

"You're bag will be waiting for you by the door, and I never skip breakfast. I prefer to eviscerate my enemies on a full stomach."

"Um… I'm not sure how literally you mean that."

"I'm very serious. Also, Lola might seem sweet and innocent, but try leaving without letting her feed you, and you'll see a new side of her."

I couldn't help but laugh at the image of her berating Lucien for skipping breakfast.

"After I lost my mom, she took over making sure Angelo and my father and I took care of ourselves, not that she has to worry too much about me, but my father has a heart condition now, and my idiot brother and cousin seem to think they can survive on coffee and alcohol."

The heaviness of his sigh had me wanting to comfort him, but I wasn't sure he'd accept that, so I tried teasing him instead. "So they're the problem, and you're a pure and good soul?"

The glare he gave me had my pulse speeding up. Had I gone too far?

I knew I hadn't when he started to laugh. The sound echoed as we entered the large dining room. "Of course I am. You must know that after last night."

"Is he trying to tell you he's smarter than God?" The question had come from Devil, who was lounging back in a chair with his feet up on another one.

Lucien slapped him on the side of his head. "Put your fucking feet down and show some fucking manners."

"He's not all that, you know?" Devil continued. "Being the oldest doesn't make him the smartest."

Lucien glared at his cousin, and I was glad that chilling look wasn't directed at me. "Don't forget who's in charge here. You take orders from me. Don't make me regret giving you more responsibility."

"Lay off him, Devil," Angelo said, entering the dining room behind us. "He's got his new man here. Let him enjoy it."

Devil snorted and gave me a slow once-over. "How long do you think you'll last here? I'm surprised Luce hasn't chewed you up and spit you out already."

Lucien grabbed Devil's shirt and yanked him to his feet. I was shocked by how easily he manhandled his much larger cousin.

Devil didn't look intimidated though, he just grinned. "Fuck. Angel was right. Now I owe the bastard."

"You and Angelo stay out of my business, and if you insult Peter in any way, expect there to be consequences. You got that?"

"Yes, sir," Devil said, his tone mocking.

"Watch it. Pop's already threatened to kick you out. You push me too far and you'll lose your place here."

He held up his hands in surrender. "Jesus, I was just teasing."

"Stop." Lucien pushed Devil away from him.

Devil just laughed and headed for the door.

"You haven't eaten anything," Lola scolded, entering the room with a pot of coffee in her hand.

Devil smiled at her. "You know I don't like to eat first thing."

She huffed. "That's no good. You need some protein to start the day."

"I do all right," he protested.

"Don't be late for our meeting this morning," I called after him. "Vinnie says he's got some news."

"I'll be there."

"On time," Lucien insisted.

Devil tossed a dismissive wave over his shoulder and left.

"You're worried about him, aren't you?" I asked after Lola had poured us coffee and we'd filled our plates from the offerings on the table. I noticed Lucien took two chocolate croissants and a cinnamon roll. Apparently, he really did love sweets.

Lucien sighed. "He's unpredictable. I don't like that."

I wanted to ask more questions, but I doubted Lucien would say more. "His real name isn't Devil, is it?"

Lucien grinned. "No, definitely not."

"And you're not going to tell me what it is."

"Fuck no. It's one of our most closely guarded family secrets."

A few moments later, Lucien's aunt Sabrina joined us. It was difficult to guess her age. She could easily pass for midforties, but if she were close to Lucien's father's age, she was more likely at least a decade older than that. She was tall with long, curly dark hair. She wore an elegant dark red dress, reminiscent of a 1940s film star. Lucien introduced us, and I noticed that her presence seemed to calm him. We chatted with her until Lucien rose, saying it was time to leave.

The next few weeks passed quickly. Lucien and I rose early, breakfasted together, and went into work. I visited my uncle a few times. He hadn't seen Jimmy since the day Jimmy had told me about the job at Distinguished Properties, but I'd told him to let me know if he did. I'd tried to contact Jimmy several times, but he didn't return any of my calls or texts. Was he ignoring me like I'd done to him, or had something happened to him? I wanted to figure out if the "better offer" he'd gotten was from one of the Marchesis' enemies.

The days passed quickly. Carla kept me busy, and occasionally Lucien called me into his office because he needed my "help." This help was usually given on my knees or bent over his desk. I was almost starting to get over my fear of someone walking in on us.

I preferred the days when Lucien stayed at the office. Every time he left on some type of business, I worried about the danger he was heading into.

Working for him was better than any job I'd had, but leaving with him in the evenings was like a dream come true. He took me out to the best restaurants in the North End, where a word from him got us seated immediately. He also took me to some little hole-in-the-wall spots. Those were my favorite because we'd sit at intimate corner tables where the lighting was low, and Lucien would talk to me like he did at home. In those places, he had no need to perform for the public the way he did at the finer spots, where he was always recognized by someone. On those occasions, he had to be on guard for anyone who might question his authority if he didn't appear thoroughly in control.

The nights we stayed in were the best of all. Lucien never failed to take his time with me, making me feel cherished and wringing more pleasure from me than I thought possible. I knew I was living a fantasy, and it could end any moment. I tried to remind myself that I had no real hold on Lucien, but no matter how hard I fought it, those moments when I had him all to myself were drawing me deeper under his spell. I wasn't going to be able to walk away with my heart intact.

## 12

## LUCIEN

"Angelo and Devil are here to see you." Carla had barely finished speaking before there was a loud bang on my door.

"It's us. Let us in," Devil demanded.

"Thank you. I'll deal with them," I told her.

I hit the button to unlock the door. The knob turned, and Devil pushed the door open. He and Angelo stepped inside. I didn't say a word. I just glared at them.

"I told him not to knock," Angelo said.

"Why do we have to—"

"This is an office, Devil. Legitimate associates come here to meet with me. You know this, and my father and I have told you to conduct yourself like a professional when you're here. You failed to do that today."

"See," Angelo said. "I told you."

Devil held my gaze, but he didn't say anything.

"You've got five seconds to respond appropriately."

I counted slowly in my head. When I hit four, Devil lowered his head, gaze dropping to the floor. "I'm sorry, Lucien."

"If you want to be part of this family, then you've got to show more respect. You got that?"

"Yeah."

I raised my brows.

"Yes, sir."

"You're running out of chances."

"Yes, sir."

"All right. Sit down, both of you." I gestured toward the chairs in front of my desk.

Angelo flopped into one, making it tip.

"Hey!" Devil said. "Luce likes his furniture."

Angelo rolled his eyes. He made a big production of standing and then slowly lowering himself to the seat like he was a Victorian matron. "Better?"

"Barely," I answered. "You said you had something serious to discuss in private?"

Angelo nodded. "We've got a snitch fucking up our investigation of Ricci."

That was a serious accusation. "Evidence?"

"Every wife, child, or niece we've attempted to approach has suddenly left town in the last few days or is locked up at home, and there's no way we're getting access without fighting our way in."

"I was all for that," Devil said. "But Angel said that didn't count as keeping a low profile."

I decided not to acknowledge that comment. I wished I could believe this was a coincidence, but I wasn't that naive. "Anything else?"

"Every single non-family connection we found…" Devil paused. "Dead."

"Fuck."

Angelo held up his hands. "Right?"

"It's fucking Marco," Devil said. "I know it is. Vinnie's

already expressed his own reservations. Let's take the bastard out."

I shook my head. "I want something concrete on him."

"Why?"

"Because if it's not him, killing him will only give us false reassurance."

"I'd enjoy it though," Devil said.

"What's the deal between you two?"

Angelo shook his head. "You don't want to know."

I glared at Devil, but he held up a hand. "It doesn't affect you or this whole thing, I swear. "

I decided to let that go for now. "What we should do is make him believe we still trust him, while passing information to everyone else without including him."

"So we'll fake our meetings with him?" Angelo asked.

"We tell him meeting as a group is too risky if we don't want his uncle to know when we're making a move. Then we'll give a little real information, but nothing significant."

"We could make a move on Sandrini's clubs since he's put himself in with Ricci. He's an easy target," Angelo suggested. "We'll keep it from Marco. If there's no leak, he's likely our man, but if there is, then we keep looking."

Devil nodded. "I like it."

I considered Angelo's plan. Sandrini had gotten sloppy from using too much of the drugs he sold in his clubs. He was desperate for someone to prop him up, and when I'd cut him loose, he'd turned to Ricci. Making a move against him would be easy enough, and it wasn't likely to cause problems with anyone else since Sandrini had already pissed off most of his allies. It wouldn't prove anything one way or another, but it would be a good indicator. "Let's do it."

"You do know the snitch could be Peter, right?" Angelo said.

Devil stared at him with an oh-fuck-no-you-didn't expression. They'd obviously discussed it, but even Devil hadn't dared go there.

Anger burned through me. "It's not Peter."

"You can't be sure of that."

"I've got someone watching him all the time. When would he have gotten information on us?"

"He could have overhead something, or he could be working with someone else. Are you checking his phone? Did someone listen in on his conversation with his uncle."

"Drop it, Angelo. It's not Peter."

"Lucien, you've got to be realistic. That piece-of-shit that sent him to us is a known associate of Marco's."

"So we find out if Marco is the leak, and if so—"

"Why does he associate with scum like Jimmy if—"

I squeezed my hands into fists, longing to punch my fucking brother. "He doesn't."

"Then how—"

"Drop it. "

Angelo shook his head. "Lucien, I need to know you have your priorities straight."

I dug my nails into my palms. My brother was right to question me. I would do the same to him, but that didn't mean I had to let him persist with this.

"Our family is my top priority. I've not forgotten that, and I won't. Have I ever given you reason to think otherwise?"

Angelo shook his head.

"I'm not going to do that now."

"So if Peter were the leak…" Devil said.

"I'd take care of him."

The thought of that sickened me. I remembered the way Peter had looked at me when I'd joined him in the shower that morning. The surprise, the soft smile, and then the heat in his eyes when he realized no matter how many times I'd had him the night before, I couldn't go to work without more. I'd fucked him against the shower wall and then washed him thoroughly as he leaned against me, dazed. I would never let anyone fuck with my family, but I trusted my instincts, and they told me Peter was truly as sweet and innocent as he appeared.

I hated the little voice in my head that asked me how I would know what sweet and innocent was like since I'd never been either. Why did I think I deserved a man like Peter if he was the real deal?

Angelo started to say something else, but Devil laid a hand on his arm. "Lay off. He'll handle it."

It was rare for Devil to caution my brother. I wasn't sure if he was working a little harder to show his loyalty to me or if he could simply tell I was near my breaking point. Either way, I appreciated the intervention. I didn't want to fight with Angelo, but I also refused to talk about Peter anymore.

"I'm trying to protect you, Luce," Angelo said.

"I know, but I need you to trust me on this."

We hugged, and I sent them on their way to sniff out anything else they could find on Marco.

I tried to go through some spreadsheets that needed my approval, but I couldn't concentrate. All I could think about was Peter.

I picked up my phone and pressed a button. "Carla, send Peter in."

Peter entered my office, and I used a remote to lock the door behind him.

"Did you need something, sir?"

I'd told Peter to always address me using sir, as I would expect any employee to at work, but I was questioning the wisdom of that since every time he said it, my cock swelled.

I leaned back in my chair and unfastened my pants. "You can help me with this right here," I said, gripping my dick and beginning to stroke it.

Peter's eyes widened despite the fact that I'd called him into my office for sex several times.

"Sir, I thought you had a meeting."

"I didn't ask you to think, I want you on your knees, and I want your mouth around my cock. Right now."

He kept his gaze on my hand as he walked slowly toward me. He stopped when he reached my desk, mesmerized watching me jerk myself off. "Kneel, Peter. I'm feeling impatient today."

He did as I said. When he reached for my cock, I shook my head. "Hands behind your back. I only want your mouth."

"I'm not sure if—"

I gripped his hair tightly, pulling him closer. "I already told you I don't want you to think. Don't question me. Just obey."

I needed him like this. I needed to use him. I needed his obedience and submission. I needed to know he would do whatever I said because that was the only way I was going to be able to keep him.

"Yes, sir." He whispered the words, and there was an edge of fear in his voice. It only made me want him more.

"Open your mouth," I ordered.

He did, and I took his head in both hands to guide him until the tip of my cock brushed his lips. "Make this good."

He looked up at me. I saw the surrender in his eyes and felt his warm exhale. I knew he was going to give me exactly what I needed.

I allowed him the freedom to tease my slit, and he flicked his tongue back and forth before sucking on just the head. Then I pulled him forward, forcing him to swallow more and more of me until I was all the way in his throat. I knew he couldn't breathe, but he didn't struggle. He let me hold him there as long as I wanted to. When I let go, he jerked back and gasped for air.

"That's good, Peter. Now give me more. I'm going to come down your throat, and you're going to swallow every fucking drop. Do you understand me?"

"Yes, sir."

I yanked him to me again, and he took me all the way down. He slid his lips up and down my length as I fisted my hands in his hair. He sucked, licked, and teased, holding me deep in his mouth whenever I urged him to. Once he tried to pull back when I wasn't ready, and I used my hand on the back of his head to force him against me. He gagged around me, but he didn't fight. When I let him go, he looked up at me. There was no fear in his eyes, only desire.

"You love when I control you, don't you? I can cut off your air or do anything I want to you and you'll let me."

"Yes, sir."

"Finish me," I ordered.

He bent over me again, taking me back into his mouth and keeping his hands clasped at the base of his spine. He took my full length, swallowing around me and humming until I couldn't hold back anymore. I thrust against him, arching my hips off my chair and coming in him, and just as I'd told him to, he swallowed every drop of my seed.

My phone buzzed a few moments later as Peter lay with his head pillowed on my thigh and a blissed-out expression on his face. I stretched so I could reach the receiver. "Yes?"

"I'm sorry to disturb you, sir," Carla said, "but Vincent Trevisani is here, and he says the matter is urgent."

I knew Carla wouldn't have disturbed me for anything trivial. "I'll let you know when I'm ready for him."

Peter had sat back on his heels as I'd spoken to Carla. He started to rise to his feet, but I held up my hand. I was about to do the craziest thing I'd done in a long time. Angelo and Devil often taunted me, saying I'd become too cautious now that I was getting old. Maybe they were right and I needed a little crazy in my life. "You're not leaving. I want you under my desk."

## 13

## PETER

I stared at Lucien. Surely I hadn't heard him right. "Sir? Did you say—"

Lucien pointed under his desk. "Now."

I glanced toward the door and back at him, my heart pounding. Was he really going to keep me under there while he met with someone?

There was a part of me that loved the wickedness of the idea as much as I loved every filthy thing Lucien wanted from me, but I was scared I would do something to give myself away.

As I crawled under the desk, I was thankful he'd gone for large and imposing when he'd selected it. I couldn't fully sit up, but there was plenty of room for me even after Lucien scooted his chair closer to the desk. He'd left his pants open, his cock out.

"You're going to take my cock back into your mouth, and you're going to keep it there during my entire meeting. Do you understand?"

"Yes, sir, but I'm not sure—"

"You can do this because it's what I want."

He'd said those words to me several times before, and he'd always been right. What would it be like to have confidence like that?

"I will do my best, sir."

He stroked the side of my face. "You'll do better than that. You'll do exactly what I ask of you."

"Yes, sir."

"When my meeting is over, if you've been a good boy, you'll get a nice reward."

Pleasing him would have been motivation enough for me, but the thought of how he might reward me made it so much better.

Lucien widened his legs as I moved between them. I laid my hands against his thighs, positioning myself so I could take his softened cock into my mouth. I heard him pick up the phone. "Carla, I'm ready for Mr. Trevisani."

The door clicked as Lucien unlocked it. When it swung open, I didn't dare move. I kept Lucien's warm cock in my mouth, just holding it there, not daring to suck or lick or do anything else.

"Close the door behind you and have a seat," Lucien said, his voice much colder and harsher than it had been when he'd given me his commands.

"I'm sorry to disturb you, sir," Mr. Trevisani said, "but I have some information I think you'll find vital to our joint operation."

"I'm listening," Lucien said.

I couldn't believe I was actually there, kneeling on the floor under his desk, keeping his cock warm. If anyone had told me I'd do something like this before I'd met him, I would have vehemently denied it, but I was hard as fuck as I sat there. My cock ached from being trapped in my pants.

Lucien stroked the side of my face. Could Mr. Trevisani

see his hand moving? Would he guess what was happening? Was this a normal thing for people in their world?

"Bozo Romano, Stefan's cousin, called me this morning. He said Marco stopped in to see him, and they had an interesting conversation."

"I'd like to hear the details," Lucien said.

"The gist is, Marco said he was back in with his family. He was pushing to get the Romanos in bed with them. He claimed the Riccis have enough allies to make a move on you."

Lucien laughed, but it wasn't at all like the laugh I often heard when we talked in the evenings. It sent a chill down my spine.

"I know Marco could've been testing the waters," Trevisani said. "And Bozo is often full of shit, but…"

"No. I don't think he is this time. Stefan called me this morning and said his uncle mentioned an upcoming meeting with Marco that he planned to check up on."

"That's odd." I could hear the confusion in Vinnie's voice. "Bozo said Marco had just stopped by, and I had the impression his visit had taken Bozo by surprise. Maybe I misunderstood."

"Yeah, maybe. Marco is up to something, though. That's for sure."

"That's my impression too, sir."

Lucien's cock began to swell in my mouth, and my pulse sped up. I couldn't pull back and disappoint Lucien, but if he grew fully hard, I didn't know if I would be able to keep him in my mouth until the meeting ended.

*You can do it because it's what I want.* Lucien's words echoed in my mind. I would find a way. I wanted my reward.

I didn't hear much of what was said over the next few minutes. I concentrated on holding Lucien's expanding cock in my mouth and not making a sound. Drool ran from the corners of my mouth, and my neck ached from holding my head at the necessary angle. My knees weren't happy either, but I would not fail Lucien.

"I appreciate you bringing this to my attention," Lucien said. "I'm going to consider our options, and I'll be in touch. Don't pass anything on to Marco that isn't common knowledge. And don't worry, if Marco has betrayed us, his life is forfeit."

"Yes, sir."

"You're dismissed."

I heard the door unlock and the sound of retreating footsteps. Then the door closed behind Mr. Trevisani, and the lock clicked. I expected Lucien to give me permission to let him go then, but he picked up his phone and made a call. "Devil?... I want you to have a little talk with Marco. Seems he was giving Bozo Romano the impression his uncle has forgiven him... No. Scare him, but that's all... Call me when it's done."

When he ended the call, Lucien finally looked down at me. I still didn't move. I was determined not to until he told me I could.

He took my head in his hands and brushed his thumbs over my cheekbones. "Such a good boy, Peter. I'm proud of you. You stayed so still. That wasn't easy, was it?"

I shook my head as much as I was able.

"But you didn't give up." I did my best to smile at him around his cock. He ran a finger through the wetness on my chin, then stroked my lips as I kept them stretched around him. "I'm tempted to fuck your face again, but I had a different sort of reward in mind."

He scooted his chair back, and his cock fell from my mouth. I licked my lips and flexed my jaw.

"Are you all right, baby?"

"I… Yes." I was more than all right. I was proud of myself for meeting the challenge and pleasing him. The way he was looking at me, like he was truly proud was almost reward enough.

"Good." He held out his hand to me. "Stand up, clear some space on my desk, and bend over it."

My legs were half asleep, so I was clumsy at first as I tried to get my feet under me. Lucien steadied me, then sat patiently watching me as I moved papers, a tablet, a paper-weight, and pens out of the way, dropped my pants, and lay over his desk as instructed. The cool wood felt good against my overheated body.

I'd been shocked the first time Lucien had taken my cock in his mouth, but that was nothing compared to how I felt when he knelt behind me, pulled my cheeks apart, and blew warm breath on my hole.

"L-Lucien?"

"Have you been rimmed before, Peter?"

"I… um…" I had to swallow before I could speak. "No." I'd never had the nerve to ask for it, and most of the men I'd been with just wanted to get off quickly.

"I like that I get to be your first." He licked me from my balls all the way to the base of my spine, and I shuddered.

"Please."

He laughed, the sound warm. "Don't worry. I'm not going to stop. Enjoy your reward."

I gasped when he flicked the tip of his tongue over my pucker. As he continued to tease me with the tip of his tongue, I gripped the front edge of his desk tightly, glad I had something to hold on to.

His hands dug into my ass, squeezing hard enough to

hurt, but I didn't care because he thrust his tongue into me, and it was the most incredible sensation I'd ever felt.

He hummed against me. "You love that don't you?"

"Yes. God, yes. Don't stop."

He didn't. He tongue fucked my ass until my cock was so hard I was sure I was going to come without being touched. All my muscles felt like they'd gone liquid.

I whimpered when Lucien released me and sat back in his chair. I turned my head to look at him and saw him coat his now sheathed cock with lube. Had he started keeping those supplies in his desk drawer rather than his bathroom? If he'd created them from thin air, I wouldn't have been surprised at that point. He was fucking magic.

He positioned me so I could ease down on his cock, and I sucked in my breath as he stretched me. I welcomed the sting, needing something to anchor me after wondering if I might float away on pleasure as my hardass mafia boss tongued me.

He held my hips, guiding me farther onto him. "Take it all."

I held the edge of his desk to steady myself. My thigh muscles quivered with the strain, but no way in hell was I going to stop. I wanted every inch of him. I wanted everything he was willing to give me. I didn't care if that made me crazy or desperate or what-the-hell ever. Yes, he'd sat right there while I held his cock in my mouth and casually talked about killing a man. That should have scared me more than it did. He was also demanding as fuck, but he'd never hurt me.

As soon as my ass pressed against him, he lifted me. "Fuck, I love watching my cock stretch your hole."

I bit my lip, trying to hold in my whimpers.

"Good boy. You've got to keep quiet in here. All those gorgeous sounds are only for me."

"Y-yes, sir." I tried to lower myself again, but he held me still.

"I'm in charge."

He sure as hell was, and I wanted it that way. He was everything I'd dreamed of as long as I didn't let myself think about the danger he'd placed me in or the cruel things he did.

He lifted and lowered me slowly. My knuckles were white where I gripped the desk. I wanted to touch myself so badly. I had yet to come after sucking him, keeping his cock warm, having his tongue in me, and now this.

"Please, sir. Let me come."

"Mmm. You know I love how prettily you beg." He lifted me all the way off him and pushed me back over the desk. Then he stood and drove into me. I scrambled to grab onto the far edge of the desk and hold myself still as he fucked me mercilessly.

He laid over me so he could whisper in my ear. "Is this what you need?"

"I… Yes. Please."

He worked me hard and fast, hips slamming against me. I let go with one hand and stuffed my fist in my mouth so I could stay silent.

"I want you to come without being touched. Can you do that for me?"

I never had before, but I thought I might if he kept up what he was doing. He angled my hips so his cock dragged over my prostate. A few more strokes was all it took. My body tensed, heat raced along my spine, and I thought I might erupt in flames. Then cum shot from my cock. I knew I was making a mess on his carpet, but I couldn't worry about that as pleasure so intense it hurt pulsed through me. Lucien drove deep, and I came with a muffled groan.

"Fuck, that's so fucking good, Peter. I swear I'm addicted to you."

It was a few seconds before I could speak. "Is that bad?"

He kissed the back of my neck. "No, baby. Not as long as you serve me this well."

"I like serving you."

"Then we're a good match."

Were we really, though?

He pulled out of me, and I thought about how hot it would be to feel his cum run down my legs, telling me I'd been thoroughly marked by him. He was right. I really was happiest when serving him.

## 14

## LUCIEN

Later that day, I met my Aunt Sabrina for lunch. I tried to focus on our conversation, but I was concerned about the information Vinnie had given me, but what really weighed on my mind was Angelo's insistence I question Peter's loyalty.

By the time we'd finished eating, I could tell Sabrina was annoyed with me. She pursed her lips in a pout that typically made men fall all over themselves to do anything to make her happy again. "You're not your usual charming self today, Lucien."

I sighed. "I've got a lot on my mind."

"It's Peter, isn't it?"

I almost denied it, but Sabrina had a way of seeing through me.

"Peter is one factor."

"I like him. He's good for you. But that worries you, doesn't it?"

"How do I know whether to trust my instincts?"

She frowned. "Are you saying the all-powerful Lucien Marchesi is doubting himself?"

"You're testing my resolve to be mannerly."

A laugh burst from her that had several people looking our way. "Lucien, it's so easy to tell you have strong feelings for him. Don't let that frighten you."

"Sabrina, do you honestly think I'm afraid of a boy like Peter?"

She narrowed her eyes, and I knew she saw through my act. "You're afraid of your heart."

I felt lightheaded and more frightened under her piercing gaze than I would've been facing any of our family's enemies. I understood the men I usually went up against. They were bent on revenge, power-hungry, but what Sabrina was talking about… I didn't have time for that in my life.

"You're wrong, Sabrina. He's attractive and obedient. That's why I'm keeping him around."

"I haven't known you to move any other attractive, obedient men into our family's home."

"Maybe I haven't found any that suited me as well as him."

"Of course you haven't, Lucien. They've all bored you after a night or two, but Peter—"

"Peter is very talented."

She sniffed. "The boy's an innocent. You've had more talented men than him, and I'm sure I could find you half a dozen right now."

She was wrong. He might be more innocent than any of the other men I'd been with, but his submission was completely natural. His skills were innate. "This conversation is over."

"No. You need to talk about Peter with someone, and I know you're not going to talk to Angelo or Devil." I started to protest, but she held up a hand. "I don't blame you, but I want you to know I'm here."

I sighed. I knew she meant well. "Thank you. Angelo thinks Peter might be passing information about our family to his cousin or even the Riccis. He doesn't trust him, and I doubt Devil does either."

"Angelo might be jealous."

I frowned. "What do you mean?"

"You've never been with a man you've actually cared about. Maybe Angelo doesn't want anyone else competing for his brother's affection."

"No way. Angelo can't think anything would be different because I care about—" I froze, and she gave me a very satisfied smile.

"It's okay to admit you care about Peter, but think about it. Angelo might think your loyalty will shift, that you'll put Peter first, especially if he thinks you're in lo—"

"I'm not. I promised to protect Peter. I care about his safety. That's all."

"Keep telling yourself that, for now, but eventually, you'll have to figure out if you care enough to keep him, and if not, you'll have to let him go."

"I'm sure we'll tire of each other before long. I'll find him a job elsewhere and send him on his way."

"How much of a choice would you give him in that?"

"I gave him a choice to stay with me or leave, knowing I'd see to his safety for as long as it was necessary. He chose to stay. When he did, he put himself under my control."

Sabrina shook her head. "God help him."

"God and the Holy Mother are probably the only ones who can."

She laid a hand over mine. "Do right by him."

I took a long breath. "I'll try."

I kept replaying my conversation with Sabrina as I made my way back to my office. I didn't want to feel anything deeper than lust for Peter. I'd never wanted to fall in love, not when I knew the pain it could cause. I'd seen what my mother's passing had done to my father, and I would do anything to avoid that hell. But I also knew I had no intention of letting Peter go, even when I feared my feelings for him were growing far too serious.

## 15

## PETER

L ucien had to be out of town again that night, so after
work, I went to visit Uncle Mac. When I arrived, I was
shocked to see Jimmy sitting at the bar. He was talking to a
woman I didn't recognize. As I made my way through the
crowd, she rose from her stool, and several men's eyes
followed her as she headed for the side exit. Jimmy made no
move to leave, so I made my way over to him. "Where the
hell have you been?"

"Yo, Peter. I've been around."

"Around but not responding to my texts or calls after
getting me mixed up in your shit?"

He downed about half his beer. "From what I hear, things
didn't turn out so bad for you. All those protests about how
you didn't want a sugar daddy, and now you're shacked up
with Lucien Marchesi."

I shushed him, looking around to see if anyone seemed to
be paying attention to our conversation. Thankfully, no one
was. "How do you know what I've been up to?"

"Word gets around. If you know who to listen to."

"Who are you listening to, Jimmy? Who are you working for, and why did you send me to take your place that day?"

He fiddled with his beer glass, not meeting my eyes. "I told you. I got a better offer."

"Marchesi didn't offer you a job. You owed a debt."

"I decided I'd rather pursue an opportunity that would earn enough to pay him back."

He was going to get himself killed, and I didn't want Lucien to be the one to do it. "Jimmy, that's—"

"Look, if you know what's good for you, you'll stay out of it."

"You're making trouble for yourself."

He shook his head. "I was in trouble, but now I'm doing real good."

I knew better than to believe that. "I'm worried about you."

"I should be the one who's worried. You're way too naïve to be under that monster's control. You're the one who needs to be careful so things don't end badly."

Was he right? There was no doubt I was in over my head with Lucien, but I believed Lucien when he said he would protect me. But how long would that last, and what would happen to me afterwards? Those were the questions I tried not to think about.

"Don't make the mistake of thinking someone like Marchesi cares about you," Jimmy said. "Men like that only care about what you can give them."

"Then why did you send me to him?"

Jimmy shrugged. "You needed a job. I found you one, and it sounds like you're making the best of it for now. You should be thanking me, not bitching at me."

Before I could come up with a response, Jimmy polished off his beer and slid from his stool. "I've got to go."

"Be careful. I don't know what's going on in your world right now, but—"

"You've made it your world too, and you're not ready to play in it."

"You're right, but you seem to think you're invincible."

He huffed. "Not invincible. Just smart."

Smart was not a thing Jimmy had ever been. He was impulsive, conniving, a charmer, and a halfway decent petty thief, but he would never be the brains of any operation. And if he thought he could outsmart a man like Lucien, he was way off base. "Think before you jump into something you can't get out of."

Jimmy just laughed. "Too late." He turned and walked away.

My uncle noticed me then. A few moments later, he brought me my favorite beer. "Whatever he was telling you, ignore it. He's in a pisser of a mood tonight."

"Do you know why?"

Uncle Mac frowned. "I've overheard a few things. I'll be taking a break in about fifteen minutes. If you can hang around, meet me in my office."

"I'll do that." I was hoping my uncle might've heard something useful. If my suspicions were right, and Jimmy was working for the man who was moving against Lucien's family, what would I do? Would I tell Lucien what I learned and put my loyalty to him over my loyalty to my family?

Did I really owe loyalty to Jimmy, though? Sure, he'd protected me when we were kids, and he'd been kind to me in the past, but he'd tricked me into paying his debt for him. Technically, anyway. As it turned out, I was happy to do it. He knew who Lucien was and what he was capable of, yet he'd handed me over to him, not knowing how he'd treat me.

"So what did you hear?" I asked Mac when he joined me in his office.

He studied me for a moment. "Before we get into that, tell me how you're doing. Don't think I've missed that you have somebody watching over you. I know you're involved in some of the same shit as Jimmy."

"It would be better if you didn't know too many details."

"I'm sure it would, and it might be best if you didn't get involved in what I heard Jimmy talking about."

"I'm worried about him. I think he's gotten involved with the wrong people."

"And you haven't?"

"I… Maybe, but I've been safe so far. Please, tell me about Jimmy. I really am worried about him."

He sighed. "You and me both, kid."

I laid a hand over his. "I know you're worried about me too, but I'm really happy where I am."

"I can tell that. You look better than you have in a long time. I'm just worried about what will happen down the road."

"Me too, but I'm okay for now."

"I like that you made the choice yourself. Part of me likes that you're taking a risk, but you need to be careful."

"I am."

He didn't look reassured, but he dropped the subject. "I don't know a lot of details about Jimmy, but what I do know is he's believing a lot of promises that aren't likely to come true. If I had to make a guess, he's being set up to be somebody's scapegoat."

"Do you know any names?"

He raised his brows. "Are you going to report what I tell you?"

"If I think it's going to help the right people, then maybe."

"Are there any good people in this?"

It was my turn to sigh. "I wish I knew."

"I heard Jimmy mention a name when he was on the phone. It was loud in here, like always, but I think he said Marc or—"

"Marco?"

"That's probably it. Why? You know a Marco he's worked with?"

"Maybe." Marco was the man Lucien thought had betrayed him.

"I heard him say Marco was moving against Jimmy's old employers, and he was helping him."

My heart raced. Jimmy owed a debt to Lucien, but had he been working for him? If so, then Lucien's and the man he'd been talking to—Vinnie's—suspicions were right. Marco wasn't on their side.

"Do you know who Jimmy was working for?"

Mac shook his head. "I don't. Problem is, you know Jimmy. He'll jump ship faster than you can blink if he thinks he can get more money from one place than another. He's got no sense of loyalty, and that's probably going to get him killed."

I agreed with my uncle. What I needed to do was figure out who Jimmy was working for before he sent me to Lucien. If it was the Marchesis, then telling what I knew might help convince Angelo I wasn't the one leaking information. I'd overheard him when he was meeting with Lucien. They'd been yelling too loud for me not to hear since I was talking with Carla at the time.

I knew Angelo's opinion didn't really matter as long as Lucien believed me, but I didn't want to come between Lucien and his brother. I felt a strong sense of loyalty to my uncle, but as far as the rest of my family went, I would choose Lucien over them any day.

Still, I didn't share what I'd learned with Lucien right away, though it weighed on me over the next few days. Without more concrete details—or the certainty that I had the name right—the information didn't really mean anything. Jimmy had worked for plenty of people, so even if he had worked for the Marchesis, I couldn't be sure he was referring to them.

Lucien seemed increasingly tense as the week went on. He was more distant than he'd ever been with me, and there was something desperate in him when he came to bed each night. I asked him what was wrong, but he said he didn't want to burden me with his business concerns.

Very early one morning, I got a call from my uncle.

"Is everything okay?" It wasn't like him to call just to chat, especially not at that hour. He usually just texted if he had something to tell me.

"Jimmy came by yesterday afternoon and begged me for money. He seemed really shaken up. At first, I thought he was on something, then I decided it was fear making him seem crazy."

"What did you tell him?"

"I refused to give him anything. I told him years ago he wasn't getting anything else from me. He's screwed me over enough by spending the money on drugs or stupid schemes that are supposed to make millions but never earn him a cent."

"What did he say?"

"He cussed me out and stomped off. After I closed up, I stayed in my office to go over payroll. I heard something up front. It was Jimmy. The asshole was in there trying to rob the till. I told him if I saw him around again, he'd regret it. He dropped what he'd taken and ran."

What kind of trouble was he in now? Had he betrayed Marco? "How did you get him to leave the money?"

"He knows damn well I could beat the shit out of him, and I had my Glock. You know I keep it on me when I'm working."

I did, and it had always scared me. "You threatened to shoot him?"

"Fuck right I did. The boy was robbing me. When he ran, he dropped a piece of paper. It's hard to make out the chicken scratch Jimmy passes off as handwriting, but I think it says DiGiulio's and then eight o'clock."

"Lucien's restaurant."

Mac hummed. "Isn't it opening soon?"

It was, and Lucien wanted the opening to go perfectly. Was Jimmy seriously trying to fuck Lucien over again? Did he think he could get away with that? "Thank you, Uncle Mac. Are you all right?"

"I'm fine. I can take care of myself, and you're welcome. Whatever you do with the information, be careful."

"I will."

# 16

## LUCIEN

When I stepped out of the shower, I heard Peter's voice. I leaned out the bathroom door and saw he was still sitting in bed, talking on the phone. When I heard him mention Jimmy, I tensed. I dried off quickly, put on a robe, and stepped back into the bedroom as he was ending his call. "Who was that?"

"My Uncle Mac. I need to talk to you."

He looked terrified, so I sat down next to him. "What's wrong, Peter?"

"I have some information about my cousin Jimmy. I think it might relate to what's going on with your family right now."

I shifted to lean against the headboard and pulled him into my arms, relieved he wasn't planning to keep anything from me. "Have you seen him since the day he first sent you to me?"

Peter nodded against my shoulder. "Once. A few nights ago when you were out of town. I guess I should have told you. Jimmy's my cousin, but he hasn't shown any loyalty to me or my uncle."

I hadn't told him he had to report seeing Jimmy to me, though I wished he had. "I don't think Jimmy knows the meaning of the word loyalty."

"I don't think so either."

"But you do."

He looked up at me then. "Understand loyalty? Yes, I do."

"Good. Now tell me what your uncle said."

"Jimmy tried to rob my uncle's bar last night, and…"

"I need to hear it all. I understand you not wanting to tell me you'd seen him the other night, but I won't allow you to hold back information that might affect my family."

Peter nodded. It took a moment, but eventually, he looked up and held my gaze. "I won't. I owe you a lot more than I owe Jimmy."

I hadn't realized how tense I was until Peter said those words. I relaxed and pulled him tighter against me. He was exactly who I thought he was—an innocent man who'd gotten mixed up with me because of his asshole cousin. At least Jimmy had done one thing right by sending Peter to me. "You're a good boy, Peter. Now tell me what you learned."

"My uncle found a note that Jimmy dropped. It said DiGiulio's and then eight o'clock."

Fucking bastard thought he was going to fuck with my restaurant. We'd put a stop to that. "Hold on. I think we might need to have this conversation with Angelo and Devil." Peter looked apprehensive. "What's wrong?"

"I overheard you talking with them the other day. I was standing by Carla's desk. I didn't mean to eavesdrop, but you were loud because you were angry, and—"

"It's okay. You do understand that I trust you, right?"

He nodded. "Yes, sir."

"Good. And you do remember that I promised to protect you?"

"But they're your family."

"And because of that they would never hurt you unless you went after me."

"But if they don't belie—"

I snarled. "They will believe what I tell them. You're mine, and I won't let anyone harm you."

"I—"

"Are you contradicting me?"

"No, sir."

"Good." I picked up my phone, called Lola, and asked her to bring coffee and pastries to the sunroom. Then I called my brother and told him to get himself and Devil downstairs in fifteen minutes.

They scowled when Peter and I entered the sunroom. We'd taken a lot more than fifteen minutes because I'd decided to reward Peter's honesty with a quick, hard fuck before sending him to the shower.

"What's going on that you needed to drag us out of bed?" Angelo asked.

I led Peter to the couch. Once we were seated, I said, "Peter has some information for us."

"How do we know—"

I glared at my brother. "We're all going to listen, and then if you have questions, you can ask them."

Angelo knew better than to argue with me, so I turned to Peter.

"I'm not sure where to start." Peter was sitting on the edge of his seat, back rigid.

"Relax, kid," Devil said. "I won't bite unless you ask me to."

A growl emanated from me, but Devil just laughed.

"Peter is off-limits."

"I'm just tryin' to put him at ease."

"Enough." Everyone seemed startled by the harshness of my tone, but I'd run out of patience. "Peter, I'm waiting. Start from the day you saw Jimmy."

"Where did you—"

Devil smacked my brother. "Shut up, Angel. Lucien's not in the mood."

Angelo huffed, but he stayed quiet.

"I went to visit my uncle at his bar three days ago and Jimmy was there. He didn't tell me anything specific about who he was working for. He just kept implying that something big was coming, and he was going to be rolling in it once he pulled it off. Later, after he left, my uncle told me he'd overheard a phone call where Jimmy had said a name he was pretty sure was Marco."

"Fucking Marco," Devil hissed. "Lying piece of shit."

Angelo laid a hand on his shoulder. "If he's been playing us after all, he's dead. We all know that. He may have gotten word about our plan for Sandrini somehow or followed one of our men."

Sandrini and his family had gone to ground before our attack on them, indicating Marco wasn't our leak, but Angelo was right, he could have gotten the information another way. "We knew that one test wasn't going to be enough," I said. "Go on, Peter."

"Last night, Jimmy went to my uncle, begging for money. My uncle stayed at his bar after closing, and Jimmy came back and tried to rob the place. My uncle ran him off, but he dropped a piece of paper. It had one word written on it and a time. DiGiulio's. Eight o'clock."

"Fuck," was Devil's only response.

"Where is your cousin now?" I asked.

Peter shook his head. "I don't know. He ran, and Uncle Mac told him not to come back."

"Why didn't you say something when you first saw him?" Angelo asked.

"I didn't know if it was relevant."

"Were you hoping to protect him?"

Peter shook his head. "He's my cousin, but he doesn't care about me or my uncle, only about himself. And I—"

"Who are you loyal to?"

"My uncle." He looked at me. "And Lucien."

"That's enough." I brought my hand down on the table beside me, startling everyone. "Peter gave us the information. Now we need to figure out what to do with it."

"We change nothing," Devil said. "We do the launch as planned and double our security. No matter who the Riccis have been talking to, they don't have the network we do. They won't get through our people, but we'll get to see who's willing to move against us."

"I am changing one thing. I'm not bringing Peter."

Peter laid a hand on my thigh. "If they know about me, won't that tip them off?"

"It could," Angelo said. "We know he's on their radar already. If we're going to continue like nothing's happening, you need to bring him. You'd never attend a function like this without a pretty boy on your arm."

I knew they were right, but the thought of putting Peter in danger soured my stomach. I'd sworn to protect him, and I could be putting a target on him instead.

"We'll use our best people. I can even call Giorgio."

"I'm not sure that's necessary." Giorgio was the best sniper in the business. He scared even me.

"And if they do make a move, the publicity will work in our favor," Angelo said.

I glared at him. "If people get shot while they're eating dinner, that will not bring us a rush of customers."

Devil shrugged. "Maybe. Maybe not. But that's also not going to happen."

Angelo nodded. "Finding out someone tried to make a move on elusive bad boy Lucien Marchesi but he foiled their attempt will absolutely bring customers in."

I looked at Peter. His eyes were wide, and he looked ready to bolt. He'd put his trust in me. He'd chosen to stay, chosen loyalty to me over his cousin—not that his cousin deserved a damn thing from him—and now I was putting him in danger.

Sabrina was right. He wasn't just a man I was fucking. He wasn't just something beautiful that I longed to possess. I'd never felt this protective of any of the men I'd been with. Feeling the way I did about him made me vulnerable, and that made him a liability. If I had more self-discipline, I'd send him to a safehouse to protect us both. But I knew I wasn't going to do that. I needed him now more than ever. There were days when I thought he might be the only thing keeping me sane as I dealt with the pressure of fending off our enemies, securing the loyalty of our allies, and making it all look effortless.

# 17

## PETER

The day of DiGiulio's opening, Sabrina asked me to have a cup of tea with her. We sat in a room at the back of the house where Lucien had put in a picture window that let the afternoon sun pour in. The rich red walls added to the warm, cozy feel, but despite that, I was on edge, wondering what Sabrina wanted to say to me.

"Is something wrong? I know Angelo doesn't trust me, but—"

"I trust you, Peter. In fact, I wanted to tell you I think you're good for Lucien."

"Really? You think that?"

"Yes. I know he's not always easy to live with."

Was I supposed to disagree? "Um… He's—"

"No need to try to defend him, but I want you to know that he needs your support tonight."

"He'll have it, but why?"

"Did he tell you that DiGiulio was his mother's maiden name?"

I shook my head.

"He named the restaurant in honor of her, and it's his pet

project, the first thing he's done all on his own. If things go badly, he's going to take it personally."

I was sure he would, but how could I help? "Won't that mean he'll just want to focus more on revenge?"

"Yes, but he's a lot more vulnerable than he seems."

I wanted to ask her what she meant by that, but her phone rang. It was Lucien's father wanting to check up on everyone.

That evening, I was so nervous Lucien had to help me get ready. He buttoned my shirt for me, knotted my tie, fixed my cufflinks, and threaded my belt through its loops.

"I've tripled my security force and brought in some of the best men in the country," Lucien said as he hugged me from behind, surveying us both in the mirror. "I'm going to keep you safe tonight."

"What about you? Will you be safe?"

"No one who does what I do is ever completely safe."

"I don't want you to get hurt."

Lucien brushed my hair back from my face. "Angelo and Devil will see that you're taken care of if anything happens to me."

"That's… I didn't mean…"

He laid a finger over my lips. "It's time to go. Don't worry about anything. Just smile and be pretty. That's all you need to do tonight."

"Should I be insulted by that?"

Lucien's smile made me feel warm all over despite my concern. "Absolutely not. I don't take just anybody with me to special events."

"Is that all I am, though? An accessory?" I immediately regretted the words. I wasn't sure I wanted to know the answer, and now was absolutely not the time to be asking. Lucien might appear calm and controlled, but I knew he was worried about what would happen tonight.

He studied me, his gaze sweeping me from head to toe. "You're mine. That's what you are."

What did that mean to him exactly? I couldn't help thinking about what Sabrina had said, that he was a lot more vulnerable than he seemed. I knew he was concerned for my safety and the safety of his restaurant patrons, but I couldn't imagine him ever feeling like I did most of the time: wary, ready for something or someone to jump out at me the way my parents' murderer had burst right through our door. At any moment, fear might send me running to curl up in a ball under the covers and refuse to come out.

"Ready?" Lucien asked.

I nodded, not sure I could keep my voice steady.

He kissed the side of my head, then laced our fingers together. "Everything will be fine."

I hoped he was right.

We said little on the ride to the restaurant. There were reporters and photographers standing outside when we arrived. Lucien smiled and wrapped his arm around me as we posed for several pictures. He repeated the same things about how excited he was to be opening this restaurant, how much everyone was going to love the food, and how much care had been taken on the design. He was at his most charming, and I was completely overwhelmed. There I was, on the arm of a man these people considered a celebrity—a dangerous one with no morals—but that only made him more fascinating.

DiGiulio's interior was stunning. Lucien had given me a tour the day before, but now that it was filled with people, it seemed even more impressive. The decor was sleek and modern, but the warm lighting kept it from feeling cold. The kitchen was open, and I saw the chef and his assistants bustling around. The bar was packed, and the whole room was filled with bright, happy noise. I didn't normally like crowds, but I felt comfortable there. There was a second floor with a metal and glass stairway leading up to it and tables on both levels. Lucien escorted me up the stairs to a table that allowed us to see most of the lower floor as well as the tables on our level.

As soon as we were seated, the restaurant's wine steward offered a bottle for Lucien to approve. Once he'd tasted it, she filled my glass and then his. "Let me know if you need anything else, sir."

"I will. Thank you."

When she left us, Lucien said, "We're having the chef's tasting menu tonight. It will include a selection of other wines, but I wanted to start with this and the calamari. The chef makes the best I've ever tasted. If there's anything additional you would enjoy, all you have to do is ask."

"Calamari sounds amazing. I just want to try everything."

He smiled, seeming more relaxed than he had as we'd made our way through the crowd. "I like that about you, your desire to try new things."

Heat rose in my face. I'd tried a lot of new things with Lucien, and I'd loved every one of them.

The dinner was incredible. Several people, including an actor and a model I recognized, stopped by our table to speak to Lucien. He continued to be at his most charming, though as the evening wore on, his tension grew. Several times he seemed distracted, and I assumed his security team was talking to him through the earpiece he wore.

Just as we were finishing dessert, I heard shouts from the floor below. "Sir? Sir! We are full tonight. You can't go in. Sir!"

A large, bearded man in a dark suit rushed toward the stairs. Lucien rose from his seat, and his hand went to his side where I knew he had a gun concealed under his dinner jacket.

Before he resorted to pulling out his weapon, a few men from his security team tackled the man and dragged him from the room.

I started to ask Lucien if he needed to find out what had happened when he held up his hand. It was clear someone was talking to him through his earpiece. I saw him tap the device to unmute it. "Yes. Follow the plan we arranged. I'll meet you there when I've finished my dinner and things have calmed down here. No need to make him comfortable, but I will handle this."

I shivered as I imagined Lucien's way of handling the man who'd dared to interrupt his evening.

The restaurant was quieter than it had been. It was clear many of the diners were uneasy. I saw several people rise from their tables as though they intended to leave, despite clearly being only partway through their meals. "Everything's okay, but I need to say a few things," Lucien told me before walking to the railing and looking out over the lower floor.

"Good evening, everyone." He had no trouble projecting his voice so the entire place could hear him. All chatter immediately ceased. "I'm Lucien Marchesi, owner of DiGiulio's, and I apologize for that disturbance. I want to assure you everything is under control. My security team is on alert, and we will have no more interruptions. I would like for you all to stay and enjoy your dinner. Everyone will receive a complimentary drink of your choice, and I hope you will return to dine with us again. Thank you for supporting my new venture."

There was a round of applause and more than a few whistles. Lucien bowed to those below, then turned and did the same to the people dining on our level. When he returned to our table, Bianca, the manager I'd met the day before, approached our table. They discussed the logistics of offering complimentary drinks and talked through a few other issues that had arisen.

"Can you tell me more about what happened?" I asked when Bianca had departed.

Lucien frowned. "All you need to know is that the attack we were expecting occurred. It seems everyone but the man you saw was stopped before they reached the restaurant."

His voice was strained, and I could tell, despite the calm he'd shown when speaking to the restaurant patrons, he was tense. "Are you sure there's no one else? Nothing else planned?"

"As sure as I can be about anything. Everyone is still on high alert, so stop worrying and enjoy your dessert."

I could tell he wasn't going to answer any more questions, and it would be a crime to ignore the rest of my orgasmically good tiramisu or to let Lucien ignore his when I knew dessert was his favorite part of any meal. The sweet cream combined with the bitterness of espresso was like Lucien's touch turned into a food. They'd paired it with a sweet white wine that wasn't like anything I'd ever tasted, but I was very eager to have more.

I knew absolutely nothing about wine before coming to live with Lucien, but at his house, every dinner was accompanied by a few bottles of wine that likely cost more than I'd spent on groceries in a week when I'd been on my own. But even after getting used to having wine every night, the numerous glasses I'd had over the course of our dinner had given me a warm buzz, which made it easier for me to ignore the danger we were in.

Lucien smiled at me, and I saw warmth in his eyes, not just desire but something more. Or was that just the wine making me see exactly what I longed for?

## 18

## LUCIEN

When we'd finished our dessert, I asked Peter if he needed anything else before we left.

He gave me a soft smile. "I don't think I could eat another bite, and I'm sure I don't need more to drink. Thank you for tonight. I've never had a dinner like this."

"You deserve to eat this well every night." I reached for his hand and ran my thumb over the back of it. "I like when you're a little tipsy. You smile more easily, and the flush on your cheeks reminds me of—"

"Sir, your car has been brought around." I wanted to snarl at the young man for the interruption, but he was simply doing his job.

"Are you ready to go?" I asked Peter.

"Yes," he rose to his feet, looking slightly unsteady. I offered my arm. He took it and leaned heavily against me. I liked the feel of him there, pressed against my side. I greeted a few people as we headed downstairs. Angelo was waiting for me by the employee entrance.

"I need to finish up some business here," I said as I

squeezed Peter's hand. "Angelo will escort you home, and I'll join you as soon as I can."

Angelo frowned, and I could tell something was wrong. "There's been another development."

I gestured for him to follow us back inside. When the three of us were in the manager's office, I said, "Tell me."

"Men were sent to infiltrate our house. I think they were hoping to find Sabrina or Devil there."

"Did they?"

He grinned. "Yes, but you can imagine how that went for them."

I could. Devil lived by the motto of shoot first and also shoot later, and Sabrina was just as good a shot as he was, not to mention her knife throwing skills.

"Devil is meeting us at the warehouse, and Sabrina has been taken to a safehouse, though she's mad as fuck about it."

I dreaded listening to her tirade, but I couldn't worry about that right now. What mattered was that she was safe. "As far as we know, the house is secure now," Angelo said. "But—"

"I can't risk it. Take Peter to the car and wait for me. He'll have to come to the warehouse with us."

Angelo looked at me like I'd lost my mind. "Are you sure?"

"Yes." I would rather not have Peter at the warehouse. He would see shit that would disturb him, but I wasn't letting him out of my sight. Unlike my family, he wasn't prepared to defend himself if attacked, and I wasn't going to let anyone so much as give him a paper cut. I didn't want to think more about what the intensity of my feelings for him meant, but I couldn't deny them.

Peter had lost most of the color in his face, and I could tell he wanted to ask questions. "It will be okay. I promise."

I finished up at the restaurant and decided, despite the attempts by the fucking Riccis, opening night had been a huge success. Our take for the evening was more than I'd anticipated, even considering the drinks we'd comped. The tables in the main dining rooms had all been reserved, but there had also been a continuous line of people waiting to be seated at the bar or one of the surrounding hightops. It felt even better than I'd expected to have such a great start to what was—at least for now—a completely legitimate business.

The night was about to turn unpleasant, though. I was going to have to deal with the men who'd tried to ruin my opening as well as the ones who'd dared to attack my home. Violating my property like that could not be handled lightly. If I was going to hold my position and keep control of my family's territory, I had to deal with the leaders of these men swiftly and without mercy, then send the rest back to their boss with a message from me that any further interference in my business or my family's personal lives would not be tolerated.

Less than half an hour later, my driver pulled up in front of a warehouse my family owned. We used it for storage but also as a meeting place when we needed to make a deal with someone we didn't want to bring into our offices. Occasionally, we also used the space as a holding spot for men we needed to interrogate or get rid of.

Angelo jumped out of the car almost before we came to a stop. I was as eager as he was to get this over with. Peter was already shaken, and I wanted to get him home where I could care for him and help him forget this unpleasant part of our evening. Ricci would pay for scaring him like this and ruining what could've been a beautiful evening for the two of us. I'd originally planned to take Peter dancing after the opening and then home where I would strip him out of the fine clothes I'd chosen for him, lay him out on my bed, and feast on him.

I exited the car and held my hand out for Peter. He reached for me, slid across the seat, and rose from the car. "What's going to happen now?"

"I'm going to teach these men a lesson."

"I don't… um… I'm just not sure…"

"I need you safe, and you're safest with me. You've known this is who I am from the moment you met me." I turned to Angelo and gestured for him to go on into the warehouse.

"Are you sure, Luce?"

"I need a minute."

As my brother walked away, I cupped Peter's face in my hands. "The men in there have all done horrible things. Some of them went to my house. To our house. If you had been there…" I shuddered, not wanting to think about that. Devil and Sabrina would've taken care of him, but I couldn't stand thinking about him shaking with fear knowing someone was coming for him. "I can't let them get away with that."

Peter nodded. "I know. I understand that you have to be harsh so no one else tries to take what you have."

"That's right."

"I really don't belong in this world. I don't know if I can—"

"Yes, you do. You belong with me, and you're braver than you think you are, Peter. You came out with me tonight, knowing someone planned to attack the restaurant."

"I didn't have a choice."

I raised my brows, holding his gaze. "Didn't you?"

"You told me you wanted me there."

"And what do you think I would've done if you'd refused?"

"Punish me."

"True, but have any of the punishments you've received truly hurt you?"

He shook his head. "No."

"Remember that. I'm glad you came with me tonight, especially since there was an attack on the house, but I'm also glad because I had a lovely evening with you. Things are going to get ugly now, and I can't let you go because the only way I can be certain you're safe is if you're right here with me."

"O-okay."

His voice shook, but his hands came to rest on my waist. I kissed his forehead and then led him into the building, wondering if he would ever look at me the same after that night.

"Stay by Peter's side," I said to Angelo when we met up with him just inside the door. "There's no need for him to watch or listen, but I won't risk him staying out in the car."

Peter's wide-eyed look made my chest tighten, but I had no choice. I was going to make an example of some of these men. Devil was already there. I didn't know what he had said to them, but all six of the men who were tied to chairs at the far end of the warehouse either wore looks of fear or anger. A few of them were struggling against their bonds. Considering Devil and I, as well as the other men who were there guarding them, had guns, I wasn't sure what they thought would happen if they broke free. Did they know how much Devil would relish chasing them down? If he had his way, he'd free them all and gun them down as they ran. My style was a lot more controlled.

I recognized two of the men—one was the bearded man who'd interrupted us at the restaurant and another was one of Ricci's enforcers. The rest looked like a ragtag bunch with no more sense than Jimmy. I had to admit I was glad he wasn't among those here tonight. I didn't want to kill or torture him in front of Peter.

It was clear Devil and the other men had roughed them up when they'd caught them. Each man had various cuts and bruises on his face and one man's foot hung at a funny angle.

"Learn anything interesting?" I asked my cousin.

"Nothing yet."

I glanced at each man, waiting until they looked me in the eye. Then I spoke to them all. "The Marchesis control this territory. Anyone else that has business here has to go through me. When they don't, there's trouble. I'm a reasonable man. I don't like to start trouble, but if you start it with me, things are going to get rough. Your jackass of a boss couldn't take down my grandma, much less me. He's sticking his nose in places it doesn't belong. And now I'm going to have to take time away from my busy schedule to deal with that. That does not make me happy. And when I get unhappy, I get mean."

Devil nodded. "He does."

"So before I bring down some justice, does anybody have anything they want to tell me?"

Nobody spoke. I hadn't expected them to.

I glanced at Devil. Fortunately, we'd worked together long enough that we didn't need words to communicate. I tilted my head toward the men I recognized. Devil grinned at me, and I was sure he got the message. It worried me how easily he killed, but tonight, like so many other times, I was also grateful for it.

We lifted our weapons at the same time and put bullets through the heads of the two enforcers. They slumped in their chairs, and the bearded man's weight caused his to tip and crash to the ground. Neither of them moved again.

I surveyed the remaining men. "Unless you want to join your associates in hell, you're going to go back to your boss and tell him what happened tonight. You're also going to give him a message from me. Tell him I'm coming for him. He's crossed a line, and his life is forfeit. At this point, he can still save some members of his family, his wife, his kids, his nieces and nephews. The way to do that is to end this war he's started. Now."

I heard a door creak behind me. I whirled around, ready to shoot anyone who dared intrude. But instead of someone entering I saw Angelo rush out behind Peter. Was Peter so horrified he was trying to run?

Angelo would catch him, and I would deal with him later. I turned back to the men we'd captured, but before I could give the order for Devil and the others to toss them in a truck and find a place to dump them where it would take them a long time to find their way back to town, a crash came from outside followed by a muffled scream.

I ran for the door, and Devil followed me. My guards would take care of the captured men. I pushed the door and stepped outside, gun drawn ready to take down anyone who touched Peter.

# 19

## PETER

I jumped when Lucien and Devil fired their guns.

Angelo had told me to look away. I had, but then, like when you can't decide whether or not to watch during a horror movie, I'd turned back. They'd killed two men like it was nothing. Lucien just stood there as calm and in control as he'd ever been.

Bile rose in my throat, but I couldn't look away from the bodies. Blood spread in a dark pool from the man who lay on his side, and the other was still upright in his chair with a huge hole in his forehead. My vision started to go dark around the edges, and my stomach heaved. I stumbled toward the door, needing some cold air, needing to run, to be as far away from this horror as I could. As I pushed open the door, I felt Angelo right behind me. Could I outrun him? I didn't have a chance to find out. I only made it a few steps before my stomach fully revolted and I lost most of my dinner.

Angelo kept a hand on my back as I hung there, hands on my knees, willing my stomach's spasms to calm.

Suddenly, I heard a grunt and his hand disappeared. When I turned and saw Angelo on the ground, I screamed. A man stood there, aiming a gun at me. Had he hit Angelo over the head with it? Surely he hadn't shot him. I didn't see any blood, and I hadn't heard a shot.

"You're coming with me," the man said.

I shook my head. "There are more men inside. They'll be here any minute."

"That's why we're going now." The man grabbed my arm, his grip painfully tight. I fought him as he began to drag me along, but he was stronger than me. "They want you alive, but you don't have to be feeling good. If you want to get there in one piece, you better fucking cooperate."

I heard the squeak of the warehouse door and dug my feet in. When I looked back, I saw Lucien and Devil.

I screamed, and Lucien started running toward me.

My would-be kidnapper wrapped his arm around my neck and held his gun to my head. I hadn't been that scared since the night my parents died, and this time I couldn't run. I couldn't do anything but pray Lucien could find a way to save me. In that moment, I didn't care what Lucien had done. I didn't care that I'd seen firsthand how cruel he could be. I knew he cared about me, and I knew he would do anything he could to save me.

Lucien moved closer, his gun out and pointed at the man who slowly moved backward, still determined to drag me away.

"Come any closer and I'll kill him," the man said.

Lucien shook his head. "No, you won't. Your boss wants him for collateral. He doesn't want him dead." How did Lucien know that?

"I can hurt him, though. I can hurt him real bad."

"And you'll be dead before he even feels it. I'm giving you until three to let him go."

What was Lucien going to do? If he shot the man, he

could easily squeeze the trigger and kill me before he died. And if Lucien's shot was even a little bit off target, he would hit me.

"Please. Be careful, Lucien."

"You should listen to your boy."

Lucien looked at me as if trying to communicate something, but I wasn't sure what it was. He focused back on my attacker. "One. Two." A sound came from behind us. The man turned, aiming his gun at whoever was there.

"Head down," Lucien yelled. I barely comprehended the words before my attacker fell backward. Lucien had shot him. I pulled myself away, tripping and falling to my knees then crawling, wanting to put as much distance between me and the man as I could. Then Lucien was there, pulling me into his arms.

"It's okay, baby. He's dead."

The world wavered in front of me. The last thing I remembered was Lucien's fingers stroking my cheek.

———

When I woke, I was lying in the backseat of a car, a blanket over me. I panicked for a moment until I saw Angelo sitting beside me. "Are you all right?"

"I've got the worst fucking headache I've ever had, but otherwise, I'm fine. Physically, anyway. I'm not fine that I let that guy surprise me. If he'd hurt you, I don't know what Lucien would've done."

"I'm sure he'd have found someone else. There are plenty of men prettier than me, and surely some of them have stronger stomachs."

Angelo huffed. "It's only because of what I've seen that it didn't bother me. I would worry if you were okay with it."

"We all could've died tonight."

"True. But we didn't, so we count it as a success."

How could he sound so nonchalant? "Does the money and power really make this worth it?"

"Most of the time."

"Are you all right, really?"

"I am." He was silent for a moment, then he added. "Don't hate Lucien for what he did tonight. Those men were pieces of shit, and they knew the score."

Were Lucien and his family any better? They were all criminals who were willing to do whatever it took to stay on top. How did they justify that?

"Yeah, we're bad guys too," Angelo said as if he'd read my thoughts. "But Lucien cares about you."

"He told you that?" I couldn't quite imagine it.

Angelo snorted. "He didn't have to."

"But you don't trust me."

"I didn't, but I do now. You gave us information that helped us tonight. We wouldn't have been as prepared if we hadn't gotten that tip, and even when that man had his arm around your neck, you tried to protect my brother. Loyalty like that can't be bought. That's the real deal."

He was right. Even after what I'd seen, I'd still wanted to protect Lucien. When I thought the man who'd tried to take me away was going to kill Lucien, I felt like my whole world was ending. But how could I love someone who could do the things Lucien did?

When we reached the house, Angelo followed me upstairs. "I really just need to be alone in my room."

He frowned. "I'm supposed to stay with you."

"Don't you need to rest?"

He shook his head, then winced. "Since I've got a head injury, I'm supposed to stay awake for a while."

With anyone else, I would've questioned how effective a guard he could be when he was injured, but I knew that nothing would stop him from doing what Lucien wanted.

He checked out my room, making sure no one was hiding there. I would have thought that was overkill before tonight, but neither of us had noticed that man hiding just outside the warehouse door. Once Angelo verified that my window was locked and my room empty, he agreed to stand guard outside.

I felt restless, but my legs were too shaky for me to pace, so I sat on the chaise and toyed with one of the pillows, tracing my fingers over the embroidered design. I was anxious for Lucien to return but also nervous. Could I be okay with him now? I would have done anything I could to protect him, but I wasn't sure how I'd react to seeing him again. My mind kept replaying what I'd seen. The blood, the man's dead eyes staring right at me… I shivered and pulled a blanket around me.

## 20

## LUCIEN

I wasn't sure what state Peter would be in when I arrived. I had no doubt the events of the night had changed his perception of me. Knowing I could be brutal and seeing me kill were not the same, but he needed my protection now more than ever. So even if he asked me to let him go, I wouldn't. If he couldn't bear my touch, I would leave him alone, but he was staying where I could ensure his safety.

*Can you even do that?*

After that night I wasn't sure, and that made me want to go straight to Damian Ricci's house, drag him from his bed, and choke the life out of him. I doubted I'd make it back out alive, though, and I didn't just want him. I wanted every piece of shit who'd allied with him, and everyone who thought to move against me. How dare they come to my home and make me question whether I can keep my lover safe?

I could send Peter to stay with Sabrina. Maybe I would, but first I had to see him. I had to know what he thought of me now.

I remembered the horror on Peter's face when I'd

approached him and the scum of the earth who'd dared try to take him from me. Peter had been terrified but not just for himself, for me too. He'd tried to save me. He couldn't hate me if he did that, right?

Angelo was standing by Peter's door. He'd lost most of his color, and there were dark circles under his eyes, but the worst thing was the defeated look in his eyes.

"I'm sorry, Luce. I was focused on Peter, not what was around us, and… I'm sorry."

I'd been angry when I'd realized what had happened, but I'd had men patrolling the perimeter of the warehouse. They should have found the man before he ever had a chance to go for Angelo and Peter. I squeezed my brother's shoulder. "I forgive you. We all underestimated the strength of their attack."

"It won't happen again."

"No, it won't. Now go get some rest. Devil will wake you in a few hours to make sure you're still breathing."

Angelo grinned then, looking more like his usual self. "If I'm not breathing, I'm not going to wake up."

"Fuck off."

He gave me a mock salute. "Fucking off to bed, sir."

I hugged him before he left, needing the reassurance that he was there, whole and alive, the one person I'd been able to count on my entire life.

When he left, I opened Peter's door and walked in. He was curled up on the sofa. His hair had fallen down over his forehead, and he looked especially young and vulnerable. At first, I thought he might be sleeping, but he stirred as I approached. I braced myself for fear or anger. Instead, he held out his arms, and I knelt in front of him and pulled him to me.

"I was so scared." His voice broke as the words tumbled out. I held him tight as he sobbed.

At least he wasn't scared of me. "I told you I'd protect you."

He sniffled as he pulled back and looked up at me. "How can you live like this? How can you do what you did to those men?"

"I promise you those men wouldn't have hesitated to kill me—or you—if they'd been ordered to. I do what's necessary to protect my family."

"And your business."

I nodded, hating the accusation in his eyes. I shouldn't need his approval, but I wanted it. "That's true. It's who I am. It's what I've been raised to do."

"But that doesn't mean—"

I shook my head. "I can't walk away. There are people counting on me, people who need my protection, family, employees, men who would be on the street or dead if they weren't working for me. You saw the worst of it tonight, but believe it or not, I do some good occasionally. And you knew what I was when you agreed to stay."

"I did, but seeing that... I can't get it out of my mind. And then I thought... I couldn't get away from that man."

"If I could kill him again for scaring you, I would." And yet, I'd scared Peter too, and I refused to let him go. What kind of monster did that make me?

Peter looked down at his shirt, and his eyes widened. "His blood is on me. It splattered on me when you... I don't know if I can do this." He was shaking, and tears shone in his eyes again.

"Let's get in the shower. We'll get rid of these clothes and get you all cleaned up."

"I can't just forget what happened."

"Maybe I can help you forget it for a little while."

153

I rose and pulled Peter up with me. "You're going to get undressed while I start the shower. Is that clear?"

"I don't—"

"You agreed to obey me. I'm telling you what I expect. Now do it."

He looked confused, which was an improvement over horrified. "Why do I want this so badly?"

"You don't just want it. You need it, and so do I."

Peter headed to the bathroom, and I followed him, wondering if I was doing the wrong thing, and I should just pull him into my arms and hold him some more. He wasn't the only one needing comfort right now.

## 21

## PETER

I undressed as Lucien started the shower. The moment he'd walked into the room, I'd known I was going to give in to whatever he asked. I wanted him to hold me more than I wanted to push him away. And there was something so intense about him tonight. He wasn't unaffected by what had happened. Even if he didn't regret killing a man, he was distressed by the attack on his family and what had almost happened to me.

My mind screamed at me not to forget what I'd seen him do, but I pushed that warning away. Because in that moment, Lucien was right. I needed to feel clean, I needed comfort, and I needed his strength.

I stepped into the shower once it was warm. Lucien quickly undressed and joined me. I grabbed my shampoo, but he took the bottle from my hand. "Let me."

When he began to massage my scalp, I bit back a moan. It felt so good. I leaned into his touch as he kept working the shampoo in with his strong fingers.

He turned me so I could rinse, then he began to wash my body. His hands moved over every inch of me carefully, gently. I wondered if he'd ever touched another man like this. Had any of his other lovers seen his tender side, the caring man he hid underneath coldness and malice?

And if not? What did that mean for us? I hadn't wanted to fall for him, but when I'd thought he might die, when he stood there determined to do whatever it took to distract the man who held me, I knew I already had. If anything happened to him, I'd be devastated, not because I'd be at the mercy of Lucien's enemies or because I would have lost my wealthy protector who gave me extravagant gifts, but because I loved the man he was inside, the one I saw in moments like this.

"Rinse yourself, then step out and dry off," Lucien commanded.

I did as he said. When the water shut off and Lucien emerged, I allowed myself to admire the gorgeous lines of his body as he dried himself. There was so much power in him, so much strength. I wanted to press myself against him and draw some of it into me.

I watched as a water droplet slid down the side of his neck, over the ridge of his collarbone, then farther down until it caught on his nipple. Without thinking, I leaned forward and caught it with my tongue. He sucked in his breath, and when I looked up at him, I didn't see the heat I expected in his eyes. I saw surprise along with something soft and vulnerable.

I was afraid to speak. I didn't want to risk breaking the mood. I didn't know how to explain what I was feeling anyway, not in words he'd want to hear. I was still confused by my feelings for him, but I wanted to touch him. I had no doubts about that.

I lapped up a few more water droplets, one from his shoulder and another from the soft vee at the base of his neck, before I looked up at him again.

I'd accomplished my goal. There was heat in his eyes now.

He gripped my shoulders, holding me away from him.

"I would've run tonight. If I hadn't been sick, I would have just kept going once I left the warehouse." *Why was I confessing this? Did I want to be punished? Maybe.*

"I'm disappointed to hear that, Peter. What did you promise me?"

"To obey you. But I was scared. I didn't want to see more bloodshed, and I didn't want to know how far you would go to protect your family's interests."

"I'll go as far as I need to go."

I shivered. There was a hard edge to his voice, and it was clear he didn't want me to question him. I should though. I should push for more answers. I should ask him to let me go. Instead, I stood there watching him, waiting to find out what he would do.

"What did I tell you would happen if you disobeyed me?"

"You would punish me."

He reached for the pants he'd discarded before joining me in the shower. He began to slowly pull his belt from its loops. My pulse pounded in my ears as I watched him. Was I going to let him do this? Would he stop if I said no?

He slid the length of his belt through his hands and then doubled it over. "I want to punish you, Peter. I want to redden your ass so you'll remember not to ever run from me again."

He held my gaze, and I swallowed hard. Was this his way of asking my permission?

"Yes, sir. But just so you know, it wasn't you I was running from. I mean… not…" Fuck. I didn't know how to explain what I meant. "Not the real you."

"The man you saw tonight is the real me."

I shook my head. "No, he's not."

Lucien frowned, but I saw that vulnerable look in his eyes again before he took my hand and led me to the bench at the end of my bed. He sat and then gave me a slow assessing glance. "I'm going to give you what you need, Peter. Lie across my lap."

That command, and the way he looked at me like he needed me as badly as I needed him, did me in. I remembered Sabrina telling me he was more vulnerable than I imagined. Right then, I believed it.

I went to my knees and positioned myself like he'd requested. It was both embarrassing and hot as fuck. Lucien's hand teased the hair at the back of my neck, then his fingers traced my spine before caressing my ass.

I bit my lip, but a whimper escaped anyway. He slapped my ass, making me cry out. "You know the rules. Don't stifle any of your reactions. You give me everything, every sound, every pant, every tear you need to shed. I want it all."

"Yes, sir."

"This is going to hurt, but you're going to take it because I told you to. You're here to serve me, and I'm here to take care of you. When you run, I can't do that. You defied me, and I'm going to make you sorry for it. Then I'm going to make you come so hard you never want to run again."

"Please." Was I really begging for him to use his belt on me? Apparently so, but he was right. I needed to forget the horror of this night. I needed him to force me to surrender. I longed for him to establish his dominance over me, to make me remember how much I liked being his.

When Lucien cracked the belt against my ass, I couldn't have held back my cry even if we weren't in private. The second blow stung so badly tears came to my eyes. I'd known it would hurt worse than his hand, but I hadn't known it would be this bad. He kept going, bringing the belt down again and again. My ass burned, and the pain threatened to overwhelm me.

"Breathe," Lucien commanded. He ran a hand over my ass. It felt cool compared to my heated flesh, but then he squeezed, and pain shot through me, making me cry out.

"Take this for me," he demanded. His rough tone made me shiver, but it also made me want to do exactly as he said. I arched my back and lifted my ass toward his hand.

He groaned. "You're so fucking beautiful like this."

I was so far under his spell I heard the slap of the belt before I registered the pain of his next strike. I didn't have time to catch my breath before he brought it down again. He kept going, alternating sides. Sometimes the blows were light, sometimes much harsher, sometimes so hard they took my breath and forced tears from my eyes. I took it, all of it, because he needed to give it to me, and I needed to serve him. I'd known I wanted a man who would protect me and take charge, but I'd had no idea how much I longed to give all of myself to someone.

Lucien cracked the belt against my ass so hard I screamed. He paused then and squeezed my aching ass as he laid a hand against the base of my neck. I felt distant from myself, almost like I was floating. The pain was there, but it was almost like I was somehow shielded from the reality of it. All I could think about was how much I needed Lucien and how thankful I was that he hadn't sent me away. He'd kept me there, and he was giving me what we both needed.

"Never run from me again. Do you understand?"

"Y-yes, sir. I'm yours. All yours. Use me. Come in me and on me. I want it all. Want to me marked as yours." Tears streamed down my face.

Lucien growled as he slid a hand into my hair, using it to pull my head up. I gripped his thighs so I could support myself. His gaze burned into mine. "Are you serious?" My mind was so fogged with need that I couldn't process his question.

"Are you serious about wanting my cum in you?"

I whined. "Please."

He growled low in his throat. "I want that so fucking much, but I need to be certain you truly want me bare inside you."

Did I? Fuck yes, I did. I'd already risked so much. I sat back on my heels and held his gaze. "Yes, I want it."

"Then you'll get what you want. I've always been careful. You're in no danger from me."

I started to laugh. I was in so much danger from him in so many ways.

"Peter? Do I need to spank you more?"

"No, sir. Sorry. I can't think. I just…"

"Do you trust me?"

"Yes. I want to feel it running down my legs. I want to feel the heat inside me. I want you all over me."

"On your feet," he ordered. I tried to stand, but my legs wobbled.

He scooped me into his arms bridal style and tossed me onto the mattress on my back.

"Don't fucking move."

It didn't matter how soft the bedding was, it felt rough against my sore ass, but I still obeyed him. I bent my knees and spread them wide, expecting Lucien to join me on the bed, but he stood watching me.

"Get the lube and prep yourself."

I obeyed without thinking. Once I found the lube in my nightstand drawer, I slicked up my fingers, but as I contemplated what I was supposed to do, shyness overcame me. Could I really open myself up while he watched?

"Peter, I gave you an order. I expect you to follow it."

Once again, his dark voice made me want to obey. Heat rushed to my face as I reached down to tease my hole. I ignored my embarrassment. Lucien wanted this, and I was going to do it. I pushed a finger into my ass, and Lucien stared at me, eyes large and dark. The fact that he was so enthralled he seemed to have forgotten that he was undressing encouraged me to keep going.

I added a second finger and used my other hand to stroke my cock. Lucien's lips parted as he watched my fingers moving slowly in and out. "That's it. Open yourself up for me because I'm not going to be gentle with you."

That was the last thing I wanted. I was desperate to be taken hard and fast. I wanted to forget everything but the feel of Lucien against me, his cock inside me.

Stroking myself faster, I pushed my fingers deep enough to brush against my prostate and arched my back, letting Lucien see my reaction to that zing of pleasure. All my reservations about him watching me disappeared as I realized I enjoyed giving him a show and seeing how it affected him. He took his cock in hand and began to stroke, never taking his eyes off me.

"Put another finger inside yourself. I want to see your ass stretched around them."

I did as he said, groaning at the sting. I spread my fingers as much as I could, loving how mesmerized Lucien was.

"Enough," he commanded. "Put your hands over your head and keep them there."

Reluctantly, I let my fingers slip from my body and released my cock. I reached for the pillow that lay above my head, knowing I would need to hold on to something. Lucien knelt on the bed between my legs. I stared into his eyes, needing to see the heat there, the desire. He wanted me.

Somehow I knew he didn't look at other men the same way. He took pleasure from them and gave it, but there was something more between us. There had to be.

He wrapped his hands around my ankles and pulled my legs up until they were draped over his shoulders. "Hang on tight. This is going to get rough. I need to claim you, punish you, make you feel."

I had to swallow before I could speak. "I need that too."

"Then take it." He drove into me. Usually he gave me time to adjust but not then. He was wild like an animal, freed after having been caged. And feeling him in me with no barrier between us, feeling the heat of his skin, and knowing he was going to fill me up with his cum, made me hotter than ever.

He pounded into me over and over, slamming his hips against my ass. He was stretching me open, filling me up, making me wonder if he would rend me in two, but I wanted it, all of it, everything he wanted to give.

"Peter, you feel so fucking good under me. I can't get enough of you. I can't..."

I wondered what words he might have said but not for long. Moments later I was so close I didn't think I could hold back anymore.

Lucien wrapped a hand around my cock. "Come for me. I want to feel your ass squeeze my dick. I want to watch your face as you let go and give in to this need we have for each other."

His words and the tight squeeze of his fist was all I needed to go over. I came, crying out his name, bucking my hips up and trying to get even more.

"That's it, Peter. Give it all to me. Let it all go."

My orgasm went on and on. When I was finally drained, I

sank into the mattress as if I'd gone completely boneless, but Lucien didn't slow down.

"Fuck, need this. Need you," he cried as he rammed into me harder than ever.

I found the strength to reach for him and hold on tight. Seconds later, I felt the hot rush of his cum inside me. My cock twitched, making me wish I was ready to come again.

I wrapped my legs around his waist and reached for Lucien, wanting to feel his weight against me.

I thought he might press his face into my neck, kiss and bite my throat or my shoulder, but he shocked me when he brought his lips to mine and kissed me for the first time. There wasn't anything gentle about it. He took my mouth the same way he'd taken my ass, possessing me completely, his tongue thrusting into me. I kissed him back with equal fierceness. I hadn't thought I'd ever be allowed to do this, and I wasn't going to waste a second of it. I slid my tongue along his and nipped at his lower lip, reveling in the warm, spicy taste of him.

When he finally pulled away, we both struggled to catch our breaths. I thought he might regret what he'd done, and I wondered if he would make some excuse and leave or tell me that wouldn't happen again. Instead, he stared at me with wonder in his eyes. "I haven't done that in years."

"Kissed a man?"

He nodded. "Not since I was in high school."

That made me sad for him. "I'd like to do it again."

Lucien flipped us so I was on top. His cock slipped from my ass, and I felt the warm rush of his cum sliding out as well. He groaned as he slid his fingers along my inner thigh, circled my hole, and then pushed inside, fucking the cum back into me. I arched my back and rode his fingers.

"You are fucking perfect. So obedient, so needy, so slutty when we're all alone."

"I…"

"Shh." He pressed a finger to my mouth. "You know you'll let me do anything."

"I… Yes." He was right.

He traced a finger through the cum on my chest and then painted it over my lips. "Kiss me again."

"Please," I begged.

He let go of my ass and cupped my face in both his hands. I didn't care that he was making a mess of me. I just wanted his lips on mine again, wanted to know that I was special enough to be kissed, to be given something he didn't give anyone else.

He licked the cum from my lips, then I sucked his tongue into my mouth, loving that he tasted like me. It was hot as hell, but then he slowed the kiss, pressing his lips to mine in a way that was almost sweet. It was more than I could bear. Lucien being demanding, I could handle. Lucien making my ass burn and my cock ache was incredible. When he fucked me in his rough, primal way, it was the best thing ever, but him being tender with me was going to destroy me.

Lucien broke the kiss. Had he felt the tears I couldn't hold back?

# 22

## LUCIEN

"Look at me," I demanded.

Peter swiped at his eyes before obeying.

"Are you all right?"

He nodded but didn't speak.

"Peter, tell me why you're crying."

"It's... I don't know exactly. The kiss. It was... I've never felt like that, like..."

"You're special to me, Peter. That's why I need you safe, healthy, and happy."

"I am all those things when I'm with you."

His words made my heart skip a beat. I loved him. I wasn't ready to say it, but I couldn't deny it anymore. "I'm going to clean you up, then I think we both could use a drink."

I sure as hell could anyway. I kissed the top of his head and headed to the bathroom.

I'd told myself I wasn't going to kiss Peter, no matter how much I wanted to, but after denying myself again and again, I couldn't stand it anymore. Not after I'd watched him kneel for me, saw him surrender as I used my belt on him, and watched pleasure overtake him. I had to know how he tasted. I wanted to do everything with him, even the things that would make me fall even harder for him.

Most people thought I didn't have a heart to lose, but they were wrong, and when I was around Peter, I couldn't close myself off like I usually did.

When my father had told me I would one day lead the family, he made sure I knew how important it was not to let anyone think I was soft.

At eighteen, with my mother gone and my father insisting I start stepping up and taking on responsibilities, I made a decision to shut the softer part of myself away. I pushed Ash away. He was the only man I'd let myself fall for, the only man other than Peter who I'd ever kissed. He'd gone to college in California and never come back. As far as I knew, he'd broken off all ties with his family. After that, I'd made the decision to avoid anything romantic. Love would only make me weak. I loved my family, but they were all part of my world, and I could trust them to help me hide the things I didn't want to show others.

Peter was right. When I was alone with him, I was different, more like the man I'd been before I lost my mom, but that side of me wasn't fit to run the family business. To do that I had to stay hard.

Could I be the man Peter wanted in private and still keep my edge? If I couldn't, I was going to have to send him away.

I splashed some cold water on my face, then let it warm up before wetting a washcloth for Peter. I almost tossed it to him and ordered him to clean himself up, but that wasn't what I wanted. I wanted to care for him. I wanted to treat him like royalty. I wanted to make him feel special and… loved.

He deserved that. He deserved the world, and that was what I wanted to give him. But I was afraid I'd been the hard man I'd become at eighteen for far too long to change, even if it was possible for me to be the man he wanted.

I sat on the side of the bed. Peter watched me somewhat warily. Did he think I was freaking out over the kiss? What would he say if he knew that wasn't it, that my biggest fear was how he would react if he knew I was in love with him? I wasn't ready to tell him. I wasn't sure I ever would be.

I took the washcloth, cleaned off his stomach, then wrapped it around his cock and stroked him a few times. He hardened under my touch. I'd known he would even though it hadn't been long since he'd come. He was always eager for me, just like I was for him. We were a good match in bed. There was no doubt about that, even if we were a disaster everywhere else.

"Come on," I said, releasing his dick. "We're going to my room. I want to sit on the balcony."

Peter frowned. "It will be cold out there."

"I have a heater, and I'll keep you warm."

"All right," he said as if I'd given him a choice. One thing I'd learned about Peter was that he didn't need choices. He trusted me in a way no one outside my family ever had. People did what I said because they were fucking scared of me—and they should be—but Peter wanted to obey me. Sure, I'd been with plenty of men who had claimed to be submissive, men who did what I said and liked it when I was rough with them, but it was all a game to them or a ploy to get something from me. With Peter, submission was totally different. He longed for my dominance.

I pulled my pants back on and dressed Peter in his silky robe, then led him to my room. He sat on the loveseat I'd placed on my balcony so I could recline while I sat out there. I tucked a blanket around him before stepping back inside to pour whiskey into two glasses. I opened my finest Cuban

cigars and selected one. I didn't smoke often, but it was definitely a night that called for one. I set Peter's drink in front of
him, and he frowned. "I don't usually drink anything strong."

"Tonight you do." I placed my glass down on the small table
that just fit in front of the loveseat. Then I moved to the railing, lit
up my cigar, took a long pull from it, and blew out smoke rings.

Peter made a strangled sound as if he'd nearly choked on
his whiskey. "I didn't know people could really do that. I
thought that was just something in movies."

"I can do a lot of things most people can't, but this is
easy. I could teach you."

"No thanks. I don't smoke. You shouldn't either."

Rather than being annoyed by his words, the knowledge
that he cared warmed me. "You sound like my brother. Sometimes he acts like a fucking health freak, running ten miles a
day, refusing to enjoy the pleasure of a cigar."

Peter looked unconvinced. "He eats everything Lola
makes for him."

I snorted. "Well, he is Italian."

Peter laughed, and that joyous sound pushed away the last
of the fear I'd been hanging on to since I saw Peter being
dragged away from me.

"What about Devil?" Peter asked.

It took me a moment to realize what he was asking. I was
too busy being mesmerized by how fucking good he looked
on my balcony. I'd never brought a man out here. This was
my retreat, the place I went to be alone. Even when it was
fucking freezing, I often stood out here and looked at the
lights of the city in the evenings.

"Devil fucking loves these things," I said, raising my
cigar then flicking ash over the balcony railing.

I turned and saw Peter gazing at me with a dreamy smile.

"You better not be thinking about my cousin."

He laughed again. "I'm just watching you. You're so…"

"What?"

"You really look like a mob boss right now."

"Is that a good thing?"

"Yeah. You're all danger and power, and you fit so well here, among all this." He gestured around, indicating the balcony and my room.

If he thought this house was extravagant, I couldn't wait until I could take him to our house in Weston. "There's no point in doing what we do if you're not going to enjoy the spoils."

"I guess not, but there's always someone wanting to kill you, isn't there?"

"Or kill my family or take everything I've worked for or all of the above." I took another long pull on the cigar and blew out the smoke.

"And it's still worth it?"

"You name anything you want, and I'll get it for you."

"I want to know you're safe."

I shook my head. "You know that's not what I mean. No one, not even a nondescript accountant who's never done anything more criminal than drive sixty in a fifty-five can promise you nothing will happen to them. Any of us could get hit by a car tomorrow."

Peter scowled at me, and I smiled. I loved that he wanted to protect me too. "If you don't tell me what you want, I'll just keep buying you gifts until I find something that wows you."

"You think I'm not wowed by everything you've done? I'm sure this robe cost more than the nicest outfit I've ever owned. I've never had clothes like the ones you gave me, and my bedroom here is about the size of my whole apartment. But I... I don't need those things."

"I want you to have them."

Peter sighed. "I know and... thank you."

I nodded. "Better. And I will keep giving you gifts because I want to." *And it's a way I can show you what I might not ever be able to say.*

"The one thing I always really wanted was a pony. I know that's so cliché, but I had a stuffed one, and I wanted it to be real. I never asked for one because I knew it wouldn't happen. We lived in the city in various shitty apartments, rarely the same one for more than six months or so. On the very rare occasions my parents had more money than they needed to scrape by, they spent most of it partying or blew it gambling. They gave me the basics, and they weren't cruel, but—"

"You deserve more than that."

He shrugged. "No more than anyone else does."

I blew out more smoke rings, hoping to make him smile. "Any man I claim deserves more because he's someone special. I've never brought a man to my home, Peter, never kept anyone around for this long. "

Peter's eyes widened. "Lucien, I don't think—"

I held up my hand. "I didn't ask you to think. I asked you to obey."

He scowled at me as I put out my cigar. I picked up my whiskey, drained it, and set the empty glass down next to Peter's. He'd only taken a few sips.

"You really don't like strong drinks?"

He shook his head. "I know it's supposed to relax me, but being here, talking to you, isolated from everything that happened tonight, that's relaxing enough, not to mention what you did to me in bed."

I smiled. His words soothed me more than the whiskey ever could. I would show no mercy to anyone who dared to make a move on my home. This place was sacred to me. I'd grown up here, loved by both my parents. Angelo—and for the most part, Devil—had grown up here too. The Riccis could bring a war to our businesses, they could bring it to my headquarters, they could chase me down in a dark alley, but no one came here without my permission.

I sat on the couch next to Peter, pulled his legs over mine, and slid my hand under the blanket so I could massage his feet. The sound he made when I dug my palm into his arch was so much like the ones he made when I fucked him that my cock hardened. I needed a distraction. "Tell me more about the pony you wanted."

Peter laughed. "You'll think it's silly."

"I have never, from the moment I saw you behind the reception desk in my office, thought anything about you was silly."

He looked startled. "Most people think I am or that I'm just insignificant."

I gripped his jaw firmly and forced him to look at me. "Peter Kelly, there is nothing insignificant or unimportant about you. You're intelligent and a hell of a lot stronger than you think you are."

"I'm not—"

"Do not contradict me. Haven't you learned what happens when you do?"

He sighed. "If you knew more about me, you might think differently."

"I'd like to say you've seen the worst of me, but you haven't. Those men had a quick and easy death. Believe me, I've done far worse. So don't try to make me think there's any way I'd find you less than worthy."

Peter started to speak again, but I returned my focus to massaging his feet, and he seemed to forget his words. He leaned back against the sofa cushions and closed his eyes.

"There's a place I want to take you soon."

"Mmmm. Yeah?"

I grinned at how blissed out he was now. "Yes. It's one of my favorite places to go when I need to think. I've been going there to sit and enjoy the view since I was a kid."

"Where is it?"

"Have you ever been to Fort Revere."

He shook his head.

"It's in Hull. My uncle has a waterfront house there. We used to visit him a lot, and my cousins and I liked to sneak up to the fort and play around. Later on, in high school, I'd hide out there with friends when we'd ditch school. It's never crowded, and it's not a place tourists go. It's perfect to just sit and see the city."

Peter opened his eyes and smiled up at me. "I'd love to go with you some time."

"When things quiet down, I'll have Lola pack us a picnic and we'll go."

He was silent for several moments, then he said, "I wanted a Shetland pony named Clover."

"Clover?"

"Yes. That was the name I gave my stuffed one because it came with a book about a pony named Clover. I read it until it fell apart." Color rose in his face. "I told you it was—"

"It's perfect." I pressed against his arch again, and he sighed. "Relax and enjoy this." For a few moments, he did. I wondered if he might fall asleep under my attention, but then he said, "My parents were killed right in front of me, and all I did was hide. I didn't do anything to try to stop it. So if you ever think I'm brave or—"

"Who killed them, Peter?" I needed to know. Whoever it was wouldn't be around much longer.

"A dealer my dad had crossed."

"Where is he now?"

"He was dead when the police found him."

He'd probably betrayed someone himself or called too much attention to his boss's operation. "How old were you when they died?"

"Fourteen. It wasn't like I was a baby or anything."

"Fourteen-year-olds aren't expected to go up against killers. No one is."

He frowned. "Was that true of you at fourteen?"

"I am an exception in almost every way." That made him smile as I'd hoped it would. "If you want to tell me what happened, you can."

He shook his head. "I don't want to talk about it. I've never told anyone else. I'm sure my uncle knows I stayed hidden, but he doesn't hate me for it."

"No one should hate you for hiding from a killer." As the words came out of my mouth, I realized I was expecting him not to run or hide from me. Was that at all fair?

## 23

---

## PETER

A few days later, Lucien came to my desk in the middle of the afternoon. It was unusual for him to come to me rather than summoning me to his office, usually for some illicit activity.

"Come with me," he demanded without further explanation.

I stood, but before I'd come out from behind my desk, Angelo stormed out of a conference room.

"Where are you going, Luce? We're supposed to meet with Vinnie and Stefan in a few minutes."

"You and Devil can handle it."

Angelo looked at him like he'd lost his mind. "What the fuck do you mean? You never let us handle anything. You always think you have to be in charge."

"Well, I don't think that today. Today, I think I'm leaving, and you're going to handle things." He turned back to me. "Peter, I said come on."

I took a step, but Angelo didn't back down.

"Lucien, what the fuck has gotten into you?"

SILVIA VIOLET

"I have some important business, and I need Peter to help me with it."

Angelo made a circle with his fist and moved it up and down, clearly indicating what he thought Lucien was going to do with me. "That's not important business."

"You're walking a fine line, Angelo."

Angelo snorted, but he didn't say anything else. Lucien turned to the elevator, and I quickly slipped around my desk and followed him.

"You better not be pissed off if the meeting doesn't go the way you want it to," Angelo called as the elevator doors slid open.

Lucien's eyes turned to ice as he turned to face his brother. "You will make the meeting go the way I want, or there will be serious consequences."

"What if they don't—"

"Then make them."

Lucien had a car waiting for us. Once we were settled in the backseat and the driver had pulled away from the curb, my curiosity became too much to contain. "Where are we going?"

Lucien smiled. "You'll see. It's a surprise."

"Do you really need to be at—"

"I don't need to be anywhere but right here. I run this business. The point of being the boss is making whatever decisions I want."

I knew that wasn't completely true. Lucien had responsibilities he couldn't ignore, especially now when the Riccis were trying to move in on his territory. But I also knew nothing I said would change his mind. He took a few phone calls while I simply watched the world pass by outside the windows. We headed out of town, and my mind raced as I tried to figure out where we were going.

After about half an hour, the driver turned off the road and headed up a long gravel driveway which appeared to lead to a farm.

Lucien abruptly ended his call as the driver pulled the car into a small lot near the barn.

As I stared out the window, some horses came running up to the fence beside the car.

No way.

Lucien was not getting me a pony.

How the hell would he even pull that off this fast?

"Lucien, why are we here?"

"You'll see." The driver came around and opened the door for us. Lucien held out his hand to me. I took it and exited the car.

A woman hurried over to greet us. "Mr. Marchesi?" Lucien nodded his assent. "I'm Cathy. We spoke on the phone earlier."

Lucien shook her offered hand. "It's nice to meet you. Can we see them now?"

Cathy smiled. "Of course."

Them? Maybe he wanted me to choose from a few different ponies. I didn't want him to feel like he had to keep buying me things, but I had to admit part of me was thrilled by it. He made me feel special, and even though he'd already done far too much, the more he gave me, the more I felt bound to him. If I were honest with myself, though, the gifts might make me feel indebted to him, but it only took his presence to hold me there. When I was around him, I forgot all the reasons why I should never have agreed to stay.

Cathy led us into the barn, and the second I saw the Shetland pony in the first stall, I fell in love. She was a deep rich brown with a blonde mane and tail, exactly like the stuffed animal I'd had.

"What do you think?" Lucien asked.

"She's perfect." I reached out my hand, and she walked over and stuck her nose over the low stall door. I scratched her ears, and she leaned into my touch.

"Her coloring is just like the stuffed pony I had. How did you know?" I was sure I hadn't mentioned those details the night I'd confessed my childhood longing.

"I called your uncle, and he told me."

I didn't know what shocked me more, the fact that Lucien would call my uncle to ask about a stuffed animal I'd had as a kid or the fact that my uncle remembered it that clearly.

"I… Thank you. This is…" I squeezed my eyes shut. I was not going to cry. "I know a lot of people would be more excited by the other things you've given me, and I do appreciate them, but this… I've never received a better gift."

"You're welcome." He laid a hand against my back. "If you can tear yourself away from Clover for a few minutes, I have something else for you to see as well."

I gave the pony a pat on her neck and told her I'd be back before following Lucien down the aisle to where Cathy stood in front of another stall.

"This is the other pony we discussed," she said. "As you can see, he's much larger. He stands fourteen hands high. Fourteen point two is the tallest an animal can be and still be classified as a pony. He's calm and perfect for a beginning rider. His name is Prince, but of course you could change that if you wanted to."

I stared at the Palomino pony. The name fit him perfectly. "He's beautiful, but I don't need—"

"You won't be able to ride Clover," Lucien reminded me. "If you're going to frequent the stable, you might as well learn to ride, so I'm getting you a second pony. I've arranged for you to have lessons here where the horses will be boarded until I can have a stable built at my family's house in Weston."

I stared at him with my mouth hanging open. It was one thing for him to buy me a Shetland pony. I knew money wasn't an issue for him, and I was sure he'd spent more on all the clothes he'd bought me, but a second pony and riding lessons? That was too much. And the idea that he would have a stable built just for me. "Do you or Angelo ride?"

He shook his head.

"Are you going to learn?"

He gave the gelding a wary glance. "No. It's not my thing."

I realized something then. Lucien—a man I'd seen interrogate and then kill men who'd tried to undermine his power, a man who stood down my attacker with no sign of fear—was afraid of horses. Yet, he was buying two of them for me.

Cathy's gaze bounced between us. "If you'd like, I can bring him out and ride him around the corral so you can see him in action. I can put the Shetland on a lead line too."

"Clover is perfect," I said, and Cathy smiled.

"I'm so glad you like her. I'm excited to see her go to someone who will really love her."

I would love her, but was it right for me to have her? She deserved an owner who would be there for her, and I didn't know when Lucien might tire of our arrangement. I would have no way to keep her if he wasn't paying for boarding. If he decided to send me away, I would lose my job, and I wouldn't even be able to pay my rent, much less take care of a horse.

But if he were arranging for lessons and considering building a stable, he must think he wanted me around long term. Surely he wasn't just thinking with his dick. He could get all the men he wanted with no problem, and he already had me. He didn't need to do this to secure my interest in him. Was he truly doing this because he wanted to make me happy?

"Can we talk privately first?"

Lucien nodded. "Cathy, would you excuse us for a moment."

"Of course. I have a class in about an hour, so any demonstrations with the horses will need to be done before then."

"I only need a few minutes," I said.

"No problem." She smiled and walked away.

I didn't want to piss Lucien off, but I needed to ask some questions. "I know you want to give me things, but this is too much."

"You told me you wanted a pony."

"I do, and having Clover would be incredible. So would another pony and riding lessons. But I could never afford the horses on my own, so I'm not sure it's right to accept them when you… When we're… What happens when you're ready to move on?"

Lucien's gaze hardened. He stalked toward me, and I moved back until I hit the barn wall. He slapped his hands down on either side of my head, caging me in. I glanced both directions down the barn aisle, hoping Cathy or someone else wasn't watching. Thankfully, I didn't see anyone around.

"I'm buying these horses for you," Lucien snarled. "And if I want to build a fucking stable, that's exactly what I'll do. You're mine, Peter. There's no moving on from that, so take the goddamn ponies and the riding lessons and enjoy yourself."

I shivered as I stared into his dark eyes. He was angry, but just for a moment, I thought I saw pain there, maybe even fear. Had I hurt him?

"Thank you, Lucien. For doing all of this for me."

He nodded. I expected him to step back, but he didn't. "You're beautiful all the time, but when you're happy… No one could resist you then. I like to keep you happy."

I had no idea how to respond to him, but I didn't have to. He kissed me, pressing me into the barn wall and grinding his hips against me. I felt the hard length of his cock slide along mine, and fuck, it felt good. He licked the outer edge of my ear, making me shudder. "I want to take you right here against the wall and not worry about who the fuck sees us. I'd buy this whole goddamn barn just to have that pleasure."

I almost told him to do it. It took all the strength I had to lay my hands on his shoulders and push him away. "We can't. Not here."

"We could. I can do any fucking thing to you I want."

I sucked in a breath.

My cock was so hard I thought it might rip through my pants, but Lucien stepped back. After giving me a slow once-over, he smiled. "Let's go find Cathy, have her give us a demonstration, and then get the fuck out of here."

I noticed he walked down the very center of the aisle and didn't look at any of the stalls. Of course, I didn't either. I was too busy watching his ass. Until we got to Clover's stall. I stopped there long enough to tell her we'd be back.

"You're already in love with her," Lucien said. Was that jealousy in his voice? No. I was obviously addled from too much blood rushing to my cock.

We found Cathy, and she brought Prince out of his stall. She rode him around the corral as Lucien and I watched. He was as obedient to her as I was to Lucien. He seemed content to keep to a slower pace, and he knew exactly what Cathy wanted with only the slightest guidance. I wasn't sure if that was her skill with horses or a sign that he would be easy to control. I didn't know enough about horses to do anything but trust her judgment.

I realized Lucien was watching me rather than Cathy and Prince. "You like him, don't you?"

"I really do." He was going to buy me two ponies no matter what, so I might as well enjoy it.

Cathy dismounted and led Prince back to the corral gate where we stood.

"We'll take him," Lucien said. "And Clover."

"That's excellent. I can have the papers drawn up for you later today and then—"

"I want to settle this now. I can pay cash."

Her eyes widened. "You want to pay for them straight out right now?"

"Yes. I'm not sure when I'll have time to drive back out here, so I want this settled."

"All right then. Once I find someone else to brush down Prince, I'll meet you in my office at the far end of the barn."

Lucien insisted I stay by Clover's stall while he took care of the payment. He was treating me like a princess, and that should bother me, but in truth, it felt really fucking good to have someone shower me with affection.

When Lucien came out of the office, he handed me some treats Cathy had given him so we could feed Clover.

"Do you want to give her one?" I asked.

He shook his head. "No, they're for you. She's for you."

"She's really gentle. I know horses aren't your thing, but you might like her if you gave her a chance."

"I… No thank you."

I decided right then it would be my goal to get him to at least pet and feed Clover. Maybe I would never get him on a horse, but I wanted him to be comfortable with them. If I could be brave enough to be a mob boss's boyfriend, he could pet a pony.

As Clover snatched up the last of the treats from my hand, Lucien's phone rang.

"It's Angelo. We've been here longer than I expected, so I better take it."

"We can go. I don't—"

He shook his head and answered the call. A few seconds later, he shouted, "He did what?"

I couldn't be sure if he was angry or just shocked.

"All right. No, don't tell him. What about Stefan?... What do you mean he didn't show up... Fine, I'll deal with that later... I don't care what Devil said... No. Jesus Mary and Joseph. What the fuck was he thinking?... Where's he taking them?... Fine. We'll be there as soon as we can."

"We've got to go."

I gave Clover's ears a final scratch and told her I'd be back to visit her as soon as I could. Then I ran to catch up to Lucien.

"Back to the office?" the driver asked.

"No, to the Weston house."

"Yes, sir."

Lucien's expression remained grim as the car headed down the long driveway. I reached for his hand, lacing our fingers together. He'd taken time away with me when he shouldn't have, and he was being so generous and treating me with such kindness. The least I could do was try to comfort him.

He didn't pull away, but he also didn't look at me. He stared out the window, but I doubted he was seeing any of the beautiful scenery passing by. On the way there, after we'd left the highway, I'd been intrigued by all the signs of spring, the new leaves, baby cows, birds flitting around in the trees by the roadside. Now I only noticed how much the sunny day contrasted with Lucien's mood.

"Can you tell me what's wrong?"

He shook his head. "Devil has taken some prisoners. It would be better if you didn't know any more than that."

His voice was cold, and he still didn't look at me. Just like that, the hope I'd felt as we stood by the corral evaporated. I knew Lucien cared for me, but I needed more. I needed him to see this as more than hot sex and showering me with gifts. Jimmy was right. I had a sugar daddy, one who cared about me, but this wasn't a fairytale. Lucien wasn't in love with me, and I wasn't going to change him.

He was probably right; I was better off not knowing was happening. It would probably scare the fuck out of me, but my desire for him had survived watching him kill a man. I believed him when he said the man would've killed him first if he'd had the chance, but Lucien had also said he'd done far worse. What might I see that would be worse?

No matter what Lucien said, our relationship would have a natural end, and when it was over, I would have to walk away. So maybe this was for the best. I needed to forget my fantasies about capturing Lucien's heart.

## 24

# LUCIEN

Not only had Angelo let me know Devil had gone off the rails again, but my father returned early from the Bahamas and liberated Sabrina from the safehouse where I'd sent her. Now I was going to have to confront my fucked-in-the head cousin in front of my father. Fucking perfect.

I'd known things were close to blowing up, but I'd had a plan even after the fucking disaster a few nights ago, now it was blown to shit. If Peter found out what Devil had done, it wouldn't matter if I bought him so many horses he could ride a different one every day of the year. He would never look at me the same again.

I thought Peter was the one, the way my mother had been for my dad. I thought he might be able to unfreeze my heart so I could love him openly, but now the chances of that were worse than ever. If Devil made Peter hate me, I was done ignoring his inability to follow orders. He was going to get the fuck out of my house and the family business.

As we pulled up at the house, Peter's mouth dropped open. At least he was fucking impressed, but my last fucking hope of hiding things from him was gone. Devil stood by a black SUV he'd parked right in front of the house. He had a gun stuck in the waistband of his pants, and instead of the suit I expected him to wear when he came into the office, he had on a tank top, revealing the tattoos covering his arms and showing that he didn't give a fuck how cold it was outside. Dressed like that, he looked even scarier than usual.

As we watched, he pulled the handle of the rear passenger door and yanked it open. We couldn't hear what he said, but I saw him jerk his head toward the house. Seconds later, a woman stepped out of the car. I heard Peter's sharp intake of breath, but I didn't dare look at him. It was Damian Ricci's wife, Elena. She was at least twenty if not thirty years younger than him, and while it was bad enough Devil had taken her, she turned back to the car and motioned for her two children to climb out. They stood beside her, clinging to her skirt. I wasn't sure of their exact ages, but my best guess was four and six.

"Lucien?" Peter's voice trembled.

"We need to go into the house." I didn't bother trying to explain. Nothing was going to make Peter think this was okay, because it wasn't, but it was done, and I had to deal with it now.

When we entered the foyer, Lola was escorting the woman and her children to a room somewhere down the hall, followed by two of our guards. Whenever we spent time here, Lola always joined us. I was glad she was here today. Devil grinned at me, looking very pleased with himself. I refused to acknowledge what he'd done. "Are Dad and Sabrina here?"

"They're probably in your dad's office with Angelo, but I don't know. I haven't been here."

"I noticed, and it's my office now."

Devil just smiled. I wanted to drive my fist into his smug

face, but he was trying to wind me up, and I wasn't going to give him that satisfaction.

I glanced at Peter and inclined my head, indicating that he should follow me. He did. At least he wasn't scared enough to insist I let him go. When we reached my office, I was surprised to see my father hadn't taken his old place behind the desk but had left it for me. My aunt was there too along with Angelo. I focused on Sabrina. "Would you keep Peter company while we have our meeting?"

She looked ready to protest, but when she looked at Peter, she must have seen something on his face that made her change her mind. She rose from her seat and smoothed the wrinkles from her skirt. "Of course. Peter, why don't we see what Lola has for us in the kitchen."

I forced myself to look at Peter. The disappointment in his eyes cut right through me, but I kept my expression neutral. "Stay with Sabrina. I'll find you later when our business is concluded."

Peter gave me a small nod before turning away. I wanted to follow him, to tell him this wasn't my choice, but begging someone for understanding wasn't something men like me did. I gave orders, I made decisions, and I expected people to accept that.

"I needed a snack," Devil said when he finally stepped into the office, holding a large cookie in his hand.

I grabbed it, threw it in the trash, and pointed at a chair. "Sit the fuck down."

Fortunately for him, he did. I felt his eyes on me as I turned away and began to pace the room. I didn't feel like sitting down. What I wanted to do was take Peter's hand and walk out of the room, out of the house, away from my life. But I would never do that. I had to fix this fucking mess.

When I thought I could speak calmly, I looked at Angelo.

I wasn't about to give Devil the privilege of speaking first. He wanted to brag about what he'd done, and I had no interest in hearing it from him. "Explain to me what the fuck went on today."

"No," my father said first. "You explain why he was left to deal with it while you ran around with your new boy. I expect better of you Lucien. You don't usually get led around by the dick."

My father had made me angry many times before, but I'd never felt the rage toward him that I did at that moment.

"Never speak about Peter like that again. He had nothing to do with my decision to leave today. That was on me. I thought Angelo could handle himself. He's wanted more responsibility, so I tried to let him take some."

Angelo glared at me. "Don't fucking pin this on me. You're the one that walked out without giving me any instructions except to do exactly what you would. Guess what? I'm not you."

"Right. You're the one who lets Devil get away with whatever the fuck he wants."

Devil slammed his hand down on the desk. "No. This isn't Angel's fault. It's not Lucien's either. I had an opportunity, and I took it. I made a decision, and I maintain it was a fucking good one."

"A good decision? To take Damian's wife and kids? To bring them here to our fucking house?"

"Where else did you want me to take them? The office?"

"Fuck no."

"Maybe I should have tied them up at the warehouse."

I was going to kill him. "You could have left them the fuck alone. We have plenty of other tactics to use against Ricci."

"None of them are this effective."

"They're also not as likely to escalate this war, alienate our allies, and bring the enemy to our turf," my father said.

Thank fuck he didn't agree with Devil. Not that I'd thought he would. I'd learned my methods from him, including the fact that the only way we involve women and children is questioning them.

"Does he not even know?" Devil asked, scowling at me.

"Know what?" my father asked.

"Why did you think Sabrina was at the safe house?"

"She told me you were worried she was a target."

"Because she wanted to be back in the middle of things." When was he going to learn how good our aunt was at manipulating him? "Do you honestly think she would've agreed to leave if there was nothing but a theoretical threat?"

"If you told her to, then…" My father paused and rolled his eyes. "Fuck no."

"Exactly. A few days ago, thanks to Peter, we got word an attack was planned for the restaurant opening. What none of us expected was an attack on our house in town."

My father's face turned red. He started to rise from his seat, but Angelo stopped him with a hand on his shoulder. "It's okay. We handled it."

"Devil and Sabrina were there, and they took care of things."

"So I can do something right after all?" Devil said.

"You can," I said grudgingly. "Today, you fucking didn't."

He huffed. "We've got great leverage, and he doesn't know we're not going to hurt them."

"Do they know that?"

Devil shrugged. "I didn't try to make them piss themselves or anything. Jesus. What kind of asshole do you think I am? Those kids are little and shit."

"Exactly, and you kidnapped them and brought them to our house. Now the Riccis, and all their allies, are going to come at us harder."

Devil snorted. "They were already gunning for us, and now they've got a reason to pause and listen."

"I had a plan, Devil. If we take out Damian, most of their allies will see the wisdom of begging my forgiveness."

"So now he'll be even easier to lure in because he's going to want his wife and kids back."

I shook my head.

"They're here," my father said. "You can't change that. Go talk to them and see if we can get some information out of them."

"I'm not talking to her in front of her fucking kids. They're practically babies."

"Talk to Elena. Have Sabrina watch the kids."

I stared at him. He couldn't be serious. "Sabrina? First, I told her to stay with Peter. Second, I know more about kids than Sabrina does."

Angelo snickered. "That's true. Don't you remember her with cousin Nina's kids?"

My father frowned, then burst out laughing. "She treated them like she thought they might explode at any moment."

"Mother of God, she was a fucking mess," Devil said. "Lola can stay with them, and I'll talk to Elena."

"No, I'll do the talking, and afterwards, we'll reconvene because we need a plan for what we're going to do with them and how we're going to head off more trouble and kill fucking Damian."

Devil stood up. "I'm coming with you."

"Fuck no, you're not."

He stood his ground. "You're going to scare the fuck out of her."

"Like you didn't?"

Angelo grabbed our cousin's arm. "Just let Luce handle it."

He jerked out of Angelo's hold. "Do you think I just grabbed her on the street and dragged her to the car?"

I glanced at Angelo. He shrugged, but I could tell that was exactly what he thought Devil had done.

Devil huffed. "I wouldn't act like that to a lady. I mean, unless I knew she liked it."

"So how did you kidnap her? Clearly you want to tell me."

"I told her if she and her kids came with us, we'd make sure Damian never hit her again."

That was unexpected. "Keep talking."

"She did a really good job with her makeup, but she has a black eye that's barely healing and a bruise on her cheek, and when one of the kids grabbed her wrist, she flinched."

"What did she say?" Angelo asked.

"She asked how she knew she could trust me. I told her I'd never hit a woman in my life, I never intended to, and neither did anyone else in my family. I told her you taught me respect," he said looking at my father.

"I want in on this," my father said, his expression hard.

"No, Pop," Angelo said. "We're not risking your heart."

"I want to break this man in half," he snarled.

I knelt in front of him and took his hands in mine. "So do I, and I promise I'll get the job done, but I want you safe."

"All right, son." He lifted his chin, telling me to get to my feet. "I'm counting on you."

I gestured for Devil to follow me. "Come on. Let's go talk to her."

"See? I'm not as fucking impulsive as you think."

I wasn't convinced of that. "We need a plan to get her out of here so we can keep her and the kids safe."

"I know. I'm thinking on that."

When we entered the sitting room where Lola had taken our guests, Elena rose immediately, placing herself between us and her kids who were playing on the floor with some toys Lola kept around for when my cousin's children visited.

"Devil and I have no intention of hurting you or your children. But we do need information. If you cooperate with us, we will make sure you stay safe."

"And if I don't?"

"Don't push him," Devil said. "Just tell him what he needs to know."

She sighed. "I can't talk here."

"Lola is on her way," I said. "She'll stay with the children."

"I don't like the idea of leaving them with a stranger."

"She's good with kids," I assured her. "She helped raise all of us, and we'll just go to the next room."

Lola entered then, and the children both looked up at her and smiled. She had a plate of cookies and two cups of milk for them. "I promise I will take good care of them Mrs. Ricci."

"I don't really have a choice, do I?" Elena asked.

"No," I said, "but you have my word your children are safe."

"I don't know who to trust anymore."

I hated the pain in her voice. If I didn't already want her fucking husband dead, I'd kill him for the way he'd treated her. "I'm no saint. That's for damn sure. And I don't pretend to be, but I don't hit women or children, and I'd sure as hell never hit someone I was bound to protect."

She exhaled, and for just a moment I saw how tired and

scared she was. Maybe Sabrina would go with Elena wherever we sent her. She needed someone to talk to who wouldn't seem as intimidating as me or Devil.

A moment later, she looked up and held my gaze, all signs of fear gone. She was strong. She would find a way to move on and take care of her children once I eliminated the major threat in her life.

"Ultimately, it's you my husband is after."

That didn't surprise me. He might not be the strategist my father was, but he was smart enough to know the importance of taking out the head of the family.

"From what I've overheard, which hasn't been much since he tries to isolate me from his business, he'd planned to draw this war out and make you suffer first, but now he just wants it to end. He's calling in every favor he can, trying to amass as much support as possible. He's making you out to be untrustworthy, a cheater, and too weak to control your own people."

Devil exhaled and pushed a hand through his hair. "And I just fed those rumors with what I did today."

"No one but the family knows I didn't order you to bring Mrs. Ricci to me. I can put out the word that I did. I'm not weak, no matter what he says. My word is solid, and right now I'm saying I'm going to kill that fucking son of a bitch."

"Will Mario retaliate?" Devil asked.

Mario was Damian's son from a previous marriage. He seemed to be as asinine as his father but far dumber.

Elena frowned. "His loyalty is questionable. He and my husband each have their own agenda. If he's made plans, I don't know about them. I'm rarely around him. I think Damian worries I might choose to ally myself with Mario instead of him. He's made it clear he'd be happy to take me off his father's hands."

Apparently, Mario needed to go on the kill list too. "Do you have any idea what he's planning next?"

"No." She glanced toward the next room where her children were. "If I did, I'd tell you for the chance to get them away from this life, but I don't. I only know that he's serious, and he's moved up his timetable."

"Then we'll move up ours too. Anything else?"

She shook her head.

"Thank you. I'm going to send my aunt Sabrina in. If you need anything to be comfortable here for now, she'll help you. We're working on a plan to get you and the children out of here."

"You allow your aunt to be involved in your business?" Elena asked. "Damian would never let a woman be anything but decorative."

"My father tried to run things the same way, but when you meet Sabrina, you'll understand how impossible that is."

## 25

---

## PETER

S ince Lola was busy with Elena and her kids, Sabrina made a pot of tea and filled a plate with some of the cookies Lola had made earlier that day. I realized I was still wearing my hat and coat, so I took them off before sitting down at the kitchen bar to eat.

"Talk to me. After what happened the night of DiGiulio's opening, I can only imagine all the things running through your head."

I blew out a long breath, not sure what to say. I liked Sabrina, and I knew she was someone who spoke plainly. She clearly had no fear of Lucien or anyone else in the family. But I wasn't sure I was ready to share what I was feeling with anyone.

"I know you may not believe me, but I won't repeat what you say. And please believe that whatever made you want to be with Lucien is real."

How could I believe that?

"His mother died when he was eighteen," Sabrina said. "Did he tell you that?"

"I knew he lost her, but I didn't know when."

"Lucien came out about a year before she died, and she was genuinely happy for him. She made it very clear to his father that the entire family would support him. It was the one thing she ever took a firm stand on against his father. His father listened, but he also began to push Lucien to be more and more involved in the family business. It was clear he was grooming him to take over. While he accepted Lucien sleeping with whoever he wanted, he wouldn't tolerate any signs of weakness. And he counted any show of emotion, any show of tenderness whatsoever, to be unacceptable."

I tried to imagine how hard that had been on him. No wonder Sabrina had told me he was more vulnerable than he seemed.

"Franco loves his sons—and Devil who's basically his son too—but he never showed them the kind of affection their mother did. And for Lucien to lose her when he was already struggling with his sexual identity and his need to be a harsher man than he naturally was... It changed him. He pushed away all his softer feelings, but I've seen glimpses of the man he used to be far more often since he met you. Don't give up on him."

"I care for him. A lot, but watching him kill a man, and now this... It's not easy to accept."

Sabrina covered my hand with hers. "I know. That's part of our world, and I get that it's a lot to handle, but I promise those men would have killed him if he'd given them the chance. The ones that came for us would have killed Devil and me without a second thought."

"How do you stand all the violence? Do you just ignore it? Don't you ever want to just walk away?"

She shook her head. "All the people I love are part of this world. You can't ignore the violence completely or you become dead inside, but this is my family. I'll never leave them."

"I would never have chosen to get involved with someone like Lucien, but what I feel for him… I just can't help it. I thought I was ready to accept that before I realized he'd involve little kids in all this. I thought I was maybe even ready to admit that I…"

"Love him?"

I nodded.

"I think Lucien was at that point with you too, but it's not an easy thing for him to admit. Buying those ponies for you may be the closest he can come to saying the words."

Did she really mean…? "Wait. You think he's in love with me?"

Sabrina smiled. "Sweetheart, I'm sure of it. Otherwise, he would have already sent you away so we wouldn't have an outsider mixed up in all this, but he can't stand to be away from you."

Was she right? Was there a chance I could have the fairy-tale? Lucien was no prince, but he'd give me everything I wanted. If only I could stop remembering those little children and how scared they'd looked as they clung to their mother.

"What will he do to that woman and her children?"

"He won't hurt them."

"Will he scare them or threaten to hurt them?"

Sabrina sighed. "Not the children."

"Who are they?"

"The wife and kids of Damian Ricci, the man behind the war on our family."

"I need to know what will happen to her."

"Lucien will try to get information from her. I can't promise he won't scare her, but I do promise he won't hurt her, and he will keep her safe. And Lucien didn't want her to be taken. That was all Devil's idea."

I remembered how angry Lucien had seemed with him. I had so many conflicting feelings. How was I supposed to know what to do? "I need some time alone to think."

"That's fine. I can show you to Lucien's room. Just don't leave the property."

"Would you let me if I wanted to?"

She shrugged. "I believe we should all be able to make our own choices, but I don't think you truly want to run. What you need to ask yourself is whether you're brave enough to be an anchor for Lucien when this all gets to be too much for him because that's what he needs."

I wasn't sure if I could do that or not. "I appreciate you talking to me and"—I looked down at the tea and cookies I hadn't touched—"trying to feed me."

"Would you like some food to take to your room? You do need to eat."

There was a knot in my stomach and the last thing I wanted right then was food. "No thank you. I'm not hungry."

She rose, and I followed her down the hall. Before she left me, she said, "I've never seen my nephew look at a man the way he looks at you. He really does need someone like you to take care of him."

"He doesn't seem to want that when I offer."

She snorted. "He's a very intelligent man in many ways, but when it comes to what he needs for himself, he's an idiot." She pulled me into a hug, then walked away. I lay on Lucien's bed, staring at the ceiling, and let myself fantasize about what my life could be like if Lucien truly loved me.

## 26

## LUCIEN

When I entered the kitchen, only Sabrina sat at the bar, sipping a cup of tea. "Where's Peter?"

"He wanted to be alone, so I showed him to your room."

"I told you to stay with him."

She glared at me. "He needed time to think. He's been through a hell of a lot in the last few days."

She was right, but I still didn't like the idea of him being out of sight of someone I trusted implicitly. "I need to talk to him."

"Go easy on him, Lucien. He cares about you a lot, more than he wants to I think, and you need someone like him."

It made me feel weak, but she was right. I did need him. "You should've seen the look on his face when he saw the ponies. He was so fucking happy. Then Devil called and everything went to shit. I should send Peter somewhere safe."

"I was going to suggest you spend a few hours in bed with him."

"Dammit, Sabrina. You know I don't have time for this right now. Elena says Damian is speeding up his timeline. I need to keep Peter safe. You need to keep yourself safe. I've got to focus on our plan of attack because we aren't going to win this."

"Of course we are. Go talk to Peter, then go get Ricci and make him pay."

I opened the door to the room I slept in when I was at the Weston house, but I didn't see Peter. He wasn't on the chaise or on the bed or curled up on the floor the way I'd found him the first night after I'd made him move in with me. "Peter? Peter, come out right now."

No response.

I checked the bathroom, but he wasn't in there either or in the closet.

The French doors that opened onto the patio were unlocked, but there was no sign of him outside. I called his name but received no answer.

I hurried back to the kitchen. "He's gone."

Sabrina jumped, sloshing tea from her cup.

"What?"

"He's not in my room or on the patio."

"He just seemed tired and confused. He wasn't angry with you. I don't think he would've run."

"I need everyone on alert. Now. We've got to find him."

"Go get your brother. I'll talk to our head of security."

I ran to my office. Thankfully, Angelo and my father were still there. "Peter's gone. He told Sabrina he was going to his room, but he's not there, and he's not answering his phone."

"Have you searched the house?" Angelo asked

"Sabrina is working on that now."

"You do realize you could be wrong about the boy," my father said. "He could've left to let Ricci know his wife and kids are here."

"No." I refused to even let myself think that way. "Peter isn't an informant."

My father's expression remained hard. "Don't let yourself be blinded by your feelings."

"I'm not."

"Son—"

"Enough. I'm going to search for him." I turned to my brother. "I need your help. The patio doors were unlocked, so I'm going to start outside." Maybe he just went for a walk. It was cold, but the sun was out. Maybe he needed fresh air.

"I'll get with Devil and coordinate things. If Peter left on his own, where would he go?"

"I'll call his uncle. That's probably where he'd go if he ran, though he couldn't have made it far without a car." Did he even have a driver's license? "Make sure none of the cars are missing. Hopefully, he's still on the grounds somewhere. But if not—"

"We'll find him," Angelo assured me.

"I'm going to take the trail that leads to the lake. Sabrina said he wanted to be alone to think." I didn't wait for any more assurance from Angelo or criticism from my father.

As I headed into the woods, I kept watch for a glimpse of Peter's gray coat and red beanie, assuming he'd worn them. I should have checked my room or the coat tree to see if they'd been left there.

I was jumpy, startled by birds and squirrels. I had to get myself together.

Movement in my peripheral vision caught my attention. When I turned to investigate, it wasn't Peter.

It was Stefan, and he had a gun pointed at me. No wonder we hadn't found our snitch. Why the fuck had I trusted him? I reached for my own weapon, but I was too late. Something hit me, knocking me back.

I stumbled and fell to the ground, reaching for my shoulder where I'd felt a sting. I yanked out the dart that had lodged there. As I stared at it, my vision began to blur. I tried to fight the tiredness that swept over me.

"Fuck you." My words were slurred, and the man just laughed.

Elena had warned me Damian was moving up his plans. Why hadn't I been more careful. Did they have Peter too?

"You're working with fucking Damian?"

He grinned. "You finally figured it out."

"Why do this?"

"Ash."

Was I already out and dreaming? What did his brother have to do with this? Had he come back? Was he part of their family business now?

"I know what you did to my brother, turning him gay, putting your filthy hands on him just because you could, then sending him away."

He'd known? He'd never said anything back then. The world wavered. I tried to speak, but my tongue seemed too thick for my mouth. The last thing I saw was the world flipping upside down as Stefan tossed me over his shoulder like I weighed no more than Peter did.

## 27

---

## PETER

A fter sitting in Lucien's room for a while, I'd needed some fresh air. The room was so like the one at his house in town that I couldn't stop the flood of memories of nights spent in his bed or sitting on his balcony. Thankfully, I'd brought my coat and hat with me. I put them on and stepped through the French doors onto a patio. Standing in the fresh air wasn't enough, so I began to walk. I wandered through a garden that was just starting to turn green again. I noticed a walking trail leading into the woods. I knew it would be best to let someone know where I was, but I didn't plan to be long, and I didn't want anyone coming after me. I walked along the trail until it ended by a small lake.

I only meant to stay a few moments, but as I stared out over the lake, watching birds soaring above and flitting around in the trees, I got lost in thought, analyzing all the pros and cons of staying with Lucien. Would he let me go if I wanted him to? He told me he'd only give me that choice once, but would he really force me to stay if I said I wanted out? Did I want out? My stomach churned as I tried to answer that question. I realized I'd been outside longer than I meant to be, so I reached for my phone to find out how long I'd been gone and realized it must have fallen out of my pocket when I'd been lying on Lucien's bed. I would just have to hope no one had tried to call me. I could only imagine how badly Lucien would punish me for leaving without it.

As I turned to head back to the house, I heard something. It wasn't exactly a shout, more like a groan followed by a thud and the crunch of leaves.

I shivered. Something was wrong. I was sure of it. Lucien had warned me that I'd continue to be a target. Why had I left the house? How could I have been stupid enough to walk this far without telling anyone where I was? I had no phone and nothing to use for a weapon, not that I'd know how to shoot a gun if I had one. Anyone coming after me was sure to be well armed themselves.

I wasn't just going to stand there, though. I needed to see if I could figure out what was going on. Maybe I'd imagined the sound, or maybe it was just squirrels playing in the leaves. I needed to be sure.

I slowly walked back down the trail, pausing several times to listen carefully. When I rounded a curve about halfway back, I saw two men. I stepped behind a tree, not sure if they'd seen me. Then I realized the man on the ground was Lucien. I recognized the other man. It was Stefan, one of Lucien's allies, but why was he here, gun in hand? He grabbed him, yanking him to his feet. Lucien struggled for a moment, then he went limp, slumping in the man's hold. The man picked him up in a fireman's carry and began walking away.

I didn't freeze like I had when my parents were attacked. This time, I was able to think rationally. If I screamed or chased after them, I wouldn't stand a chance against Stefan.

My best hope for helping Lucien was to get back to the house.

Why hadn't I remembered my phone? If I had it, I could call for help. Stefan headed down a side trail. I had no idea where it led, but hopefully, Angelo and Devil would.

I walked carefully until Stefan and Lucien were out of sight, then I began to run.

# 28

## LUCIEN

Stefan delivered another kick to my abdomen. I tried to move away, but my hands and feet were tied, and my brain was still foggy from whatever he'd used to knock me out. I nearly bit through my lip, trying to hold in a shout. He took hold of my hair and dragged me up. "Ready to talk?" I tried to spit on him, but my mouth was so dry it was ineffective. He slapped me, making my head ring and my vision blur.

Had he really told me this was all because of Ash? He'd known Ash and I were together, but he'd waited fifteen years to do something about it? No way. "What the fuck are you doing with this bastard?" I gestured toward Damian Ricci who sat on a chair in the corner of the cell where they'd placed me.

"Getting long awaited revenge. You've always thought you were better than everyone else. Always thought you could have whatever you wanted, even my fucking brother. Our family finally has a chance to take you down. My father was too weak to do it, so I'm making my own choices."

I'd never hurt Ash, and I sure as hell hadn't turned him

gay, but I didn't owe this bastard an explanation. "Did you bother to ask Ash what he wants?"

"Don't say his fucking name," Stefan yelled.

"Enough." Damian banged his cane on the floor.

I tried to focus on the old man, but I had to blink several times to make my eyes work properly. As much as I wanted to goad him and Stefan, I needed to survive this interrogation and figure out how to escape. I had no intention of dying here.

"Mr. Marchesi, nice of you to allow yourself to be captured so easily," Damian said.

"Fuck off." Okay, so much for making this easier on myself.

Stefan kicked me again, and I barely managed to keep the contents of my stomach down.

I opened my eyes to see Damian, standing now and glaring down at me. "Show some respect when you're in my house."

House? Surely I wasn't in town. I must be at his estate. I glanced around as if I hadn't a care in the world besides assessing the decor of the damp, cinder block cell.

"Nice basement. I guess it's convenient to keep prisoners here so you can enjoy beating them on your weekends off."

He glared at me. "I didn't say which home. You could be anywhere."

He had several other properties I was aware of, but I couldn't have been taken far before I woke up.

*What if he dosed you again?*

No, I was sure he hadn't. I was groggy but not like I would be if they'd kept me out for hours or days. Devil had been kept like that once, and it had taken days for him to seem like himself again.

I wasn't about to give away any of my analysis, though,

so I just shrugged. It hurt like hell where my ribs were bruised—or possibly broken—from Stefan's kicks, but I didn't let that show on my face. "It doesn't matter where I am. What matters is figuring out what you want and how you think you're going to get it."

"I will get it, because if I don't, I'm going to keep bringing in the people you love and killing them in front of you."

"Don't you think my family will have stepped up security now that they know you've taken me?"

"They didn't help you the night one of my men took your precious Peter. You had to rescue him yourself. If your security force was any good, they wouldn't have let you out of their sight today."

"I chose to go out alone because I'm not afraid of pieces of shit like you."

Stefan moved like he was going to hit me again, but Damian shook his head. "I'll let you deal with his insults after I'm done talking to him. I need him lucid right now so he fully understands what I'm telling him."

I fully understood that this man was going to die and Stefan along with him. I would find a way out of this. I needed to know if they had Peter or anyone else who was under my protection.

"So, you've got a plan? Something that's going to make me… what? Turn over my kingdom to you?"

"I do. People think you're cold and hard, but you have weaknesses. Your brother, your cousin, and the pretty boy you're quite taken with."

He was right, and I hated it, but I was used to pretending I didn't care about anyone or anything.

"My brother and my cousin are useful to me. And Peter

has been quite entertaining, but you have weaknesses too, like your beautiful young wife and those precious children."

He slammed his fist against the wall. "Where are they?"

I shook my head. "I don't know. They could have been taken anywhere while you've had me here."

"You know where they would be taken because you give the orders."

"Not when I'm unconscious. My brother or my father make decisions in my absence. My father is back, you know, and he's not pleased with your behavior." Damian and my father had clashed numerous times, and my father had easily come out on top every time.

"I'm not scared of him. He's old, he's got a bad heart, and I have more allies now than I've ever had because of things you and your father have done."

I hated that he was right about that too. He'd done an excellent job of pulling in people my family had pissed off, including Stefan, apparently. The cleanup from this was going to take a damn long time. But first I had to get out of here, kill Damian, and then we could proceed from there.

"Are you ready to cooperate?"

"And by that, you mean…"

"Hand over your businesses to me."

"After which you'll kill me anyway."

"There have to be some sacrifices in a war. You know that as well as anyone. I can't leave you alive to go back and help your family attempt to rise to power again."

I tugged at the ropes that bound my hands. It was going to hurt like hell, but I could get out of them. I just needed to make them leave the room so I could.

"I'm not telling you a fucking thing."

He smiled, the fucking bastard. "I think I'll bring your

aunt Sabrina to you first. Maybe I'll entertain myself with her before I kill her."

I kept my face stoic. I wasn't going to give him the satisfaction of a reaction. Years ago, he'd asked Sabrina out. When she'd refused, he'd gotten aggressive, and she'd quickly put him in his place. If she got her hands on him now, she'd tear him apart. As much as I wanted to kill Damian myself, the thought of him dying by a woman's hand made me have to fight back a smile.

Damian was clearly displeased with my lack of concern for my aunt. "I could start with Peter. You've really fallen under his spell, haven't you?"

I refused to respond.

"Are you so sure he's loyal to you? What if I told you he's been feeding me information? How do you think we found you so easily today? Maybe I should order him to end you, rather than having you watch him die. That might be the best entertainment I've had in years."

For just a moment, I began to doubt myself. What if I were wrong about Peter? I'd been wrong about Stefan and Marco. Maybe my instincts weren't any good anymore. Then I thought about Peter telling me not to risk myself to save him. I thought about him petting Clover. I was not wrong about him. Damian was trying to manipulate me. I'd been on the other side of this game plenty of times. Peter was not working for him, but the thought of him being told to kill me, knowing whether he did it or not he would die, made me long to be able to rip through my bindings and choke the life out of Damian.

Damian's phone chimed. He glanced at it, then slid it back into his pocket. "I have a dinner engagement. Think about what I've said. Imagine the rest of your family dying in front of you while you wait for your little traitor to slice your throat. When I return, that will be your last chance to save them."

"I'm going to think about how satisfying it will be to watch you die."

He didn't acknowledge my comment. "Stefan, teach him the importance of respecting me, but remember, we need him alive."

I braced myself for more pain.

## 29

## PETER

A ngelo was headed my way as I ran toward the house.
"Did you see Lucien?"

I nodded, trying to catch my breath enough to speak. "Stefan took him."

"Took him where?"

"No… Stefan must be working for the Riccis. He had a gun, he… Lucien was on the ground."

"Wait, are you saying…?"

"I don't know how hurt Lucien is, but Stefan has him. He carried him off."

"That motherfucking sack of shit. He's dead. He's so fucking dead. And all along I thought it was Marco, and that weaselly son of a bitch was betraying us."

"I'm so sorry I didn't do more. I wanted to chase after them, but I didn't have a gun, and I can't—"

Angelo laid a hand on my shoulder. "It's okay. If you'd done that, you'd be dead."

"I just want Lucien to be all right."

He nodded. "He will. They won't kill him until they get what they want from us. Come on."

He called Devil as we raced back to the house.

I was shocked they let me join them as we all congregated in the kitchen to make a plan to get Lucien back. "It's my fault," Devil said. "Stefan called me, asking when the next step of the plan would be implemented. I told him I was out of town for a few days. He must have guessed I meant here."

"It's not your fault," Sabrina assured him.

"I'm also the one who pushed him to think Marco was the fucking snitch."

"No, that was me too. I said my uncle overheard Jimmy use the name Marco but really my uncle wasn't sure of the name, but he thought that was probably it."

"Fuck. Could it have been Mario?" Angelo asked. "That's Ricci's son."

"He and Stefan worked together running the Romano's escort service for a while," Devil said.

Lucien's father nodded. "They sure did, the sons of bitches. Find them both."

"We will, Pop," Angelo assured him as his phone began to ring. He glanced at it. "It's Marco."

"Fucking answer it already," his dad said.

"Angelo…No…Stefan has turned on us…Meet us in town in two hours…We're making a move tonight…More details then but things have gotten serious." He ended the call.

"We need to contact Vinnie unless there's any reason to doubt his loyalty."

No one spoke up.

"All right. We'll trust him cautiously for now." They continued to make plans to search for Lucien and pull their allies together to make a strike. Elena and her children were already on their way to a safehouse out of state.

Lucien's father suggested Sabrina and I stay in Weston, but we both insisted on returning to town with everyone else. I spent the night alone in Lucien's bed, burying my face in his pillow and breathing in his scent as I lay there, unable to sleep, thinking of all the horrible things that could be happening to him and praying he was still alive.

His family continued to insist Damian wouldn't kill Lucien until either he had agreed to surrender the family's position of power—which would never happen—or they used him to get Angelo or Devil to surrender. But how sure could they really be?

While I was thankful that no one suggested I'd set Lucien up—something I'd feared—Sabrina was the only one who would give me any information about what was happening, and the rest of them weren't even telling her everything, something she'd ranted about at length. All I knew for sure was that Angelo had been given a place and time to meet Damian and surrender control of their empire in exchange for Lucien.

"Will Angelo and Devil go to the meet-up?"

Sabrina laughed. "If they do, it will be with a plan to kill Damian and all his allies."

"But if they don't—"

Sabrina frowned. "Damian will never let Lucien go. Our allies would never accept his authority if Lucien was still alive. The only way he's going to survive is if we rescue him."

My stomach flip-flopped. "D-do we know he's alive now?"

Sabrina crossed herself as she shook her head. "All we can do is pray. Angelo has demanded proof, but so far he's been ignored."

I hugged her, and we clung to each other for several moments before she went in search of a drink.

The sun was beginning to go down as I paced on Lucien's balcony. My phone rang, startling me. I didn't recognize the number, but I couldn't ignore it. If there was any chance it had to do with Lucien… "Hello?"

"Pete. It's Jimmy." His voice sounded strained and weak.

"What are you doing calling me?"

"I know I made a mistake."

"A mistake? You're working for people who want to kill me and—" I'd almost said "the man I love."

"I know, but please, you've got to listen to me." He coughed. The wheezing emanating from him didn't sound good at all, but I couldn't let myself feel sorry for him.

"I have no reason to listen to you. All you've done is lie to me."

A few seconds of silence passed, then he said, "I got away."

"What do you mean? Got away from who? Mario?"

"Yeah and… Stefan. They…" He paused and seemed to be trying to catch his breath. "They were never going to cut me in. Then I wouldn't… They're selling little girls, Pete. That's what they wanted me to do. Can't do that. They tried to kill me."

At least he had some lines he wouldn't cross. When would he learn to stop listening to fucking bullshit promises? "I'm glad you got away, but I'm done talking to you—"

"Don't hang up. I know where Lucien is, and he'll die if someone doesn't find him."

I couldn't trust him, but I also couldn't bring myself to hang up. "Where is he?"

"I have the key. Meet me, and I'll give it to you."

"No fucking way. You bring it here."

He had another coughing fit. "Marchesi's guards will kill me."

"I'm not falling for more of your shit, Jimmy."

"It's not…" He paused to draw in a raspy breath. I could tell he was in pain, but that didn't mean he was telling the truth about any of this. "I swear. I can help you."

I sighed. If there was any chance he was serious, I had to follow through because there was one thing I was sure he wasn't lying about. Damian was going to kill Lucien if we didn't find him soon. "Where do you want to meet?"

"You know the warehouse where they took Damian's men?"

"You mean where I was nearly captured?"

"Yeah. There's a pawn shop down the street. Meet me there at ten tonight." Was there any chance this wasn't a trap?

"You know I can't come alone, right?"

"You have to. None of Lucien's men will let me live long enough to listen to me. I'm probably going to die anyway, but I want to save you and Lucien first."

I'd never heard Jimmy sound so defeated, but I also knew he was really good at acting. All of it, even the weak voice, could be a ploy to make me feel sympathetic so he could lure me in. After what happened to Lucien, there was no way I was going to be able to walk out of there and go somewhere on my own. I was going to have to tell someone—probably Angelo—about Jimmy's call, then convince them to go meet him with me. But what if they wouldn't go?

My heart pounded. Was I brave enough to sneak out and go on my own? Brave enough or stupid enough? I was sure Lucien would say it was the latter.

But I had to take any chance I could to save him. That's

what he would do for me, and if he hadn't needed to come looking for me, he wouldn't be Damian's prisoner right now. This was my chance to prove I wasn't a fucking coward.

"I'll be there."

"I swear to you," Jimmy said, "I'm telling the truth this time. I know you don't have any reason to trust me. Lucien gave me a chance, and I blew it. He could've roughed me up or killed me. He could've done anything he wanted to me, but he gave me a chance to work off my debt. I should've taken it."

"Yeah, you should have." Except then, I would never have met Lucien and never fallen in love with him. My life might've been easier in some ways, but I wouldn't change what had happened, even knowing who Lucien was and how dangerous it would be to be with him.

"These men don't care about anything or anyone. No matter what they say, they're not going to let Lucien or anyone close to him live. I know you don't trust me, but don't trust them either."

"I won't. I promise."

That night, I dressed in dark clothing and got ready to go meet Jimmy. I waffled back-and-forth several times on whether I should try to slip out on my own or tell someone. Who would it be? Sabrina? Angelo? Devil? If I went alone and it was a trap, they'd have me and Lucien. But if it wasn't and whoever I told denied me the right to go, Lucien might die because I didn't take action, just like my parents. I wouldn't be able to live with myself then.

From the first day I'd met Lucien, I'd told him I wasn't brave enough to be with him, but when I saw that man carrying him away and realized he was unconscious and unable to fight, I'd known right then that no matter what Lucien did or who he was, I loved him, and I wanted to be with him. That meant I was going to have to be brave enough to save him. Lucien thought it had taken courage to warn him to be careful when I'd nearly been kidnapped, but I hadn't had to take any action. This time, I had to make the choice to walk into danger, and I was going to do it.

I considered trying to find a way down directly from Lucien's room, but I knew there were guards outside who would likely find such movement far more suspicious than my leaving by a side door. I also doubted I could manage the climb without injuring myself. I would just have to pray I didn't run into anyone. As far as I knew, Angelo and Devil were away from home, coordinating the search for Lucien.

Lucien's father went to bed early, but I wasn't sure if he was able to sleep any better than I had been. I was most likely to run into Sabrina. Hopefully she was in her room.

I slipped from Lucien's room and hurried down the hall. I paused before reaching the stairs and listened. I didn't hear anyone moving around, so I went down the stairs quickly, thankful for the thick carpeting that muffled my steps. When I reached the ground floor, I paused again. I still didn't hear anyone. Instead of using the front door, I headed toward the side entrance by the kitchen. I'd be closest to the garage there. I'd pocketed Lucien's keys since walking to catch the T would be suspicious.

I made it almost to the garage before a hand clamped down on my shoulder. I jumped and turned to see Angelo scowling at me.

"Where do you think you're going?"

Did I lie or tell the truth? The chance that Angelo would let me go out on my own was slim no matter what I said. I was going to have to convince him it was worth finding out what Jimmy knew and whether he actually had a key that could free Lucien.

"I got a call from Jimmy. He says the man he was working for was planning to kill him, but he escaped. He claims to know where Lucien is and to have a key that would free him. He asked me to meet him tonight at ten. I know he may be lying, but I have to find out, and—" Tears threatened to come, and my words became too choked for Angelo to understand.

"Why the fuck didn't you tell me about this as soon as you found out?"

"He told me to come alone, but I was also afraid you wouldn't believe me, and if you didn't let me go, we'd never find Lucien, and he would die. I don't trust Jimmy, and I swear I've never been working with him. I love your brother, and I would do anything to save him, no matter how dangerous." I squeezed my eyes shut. I didn't want to cry and didn't want to have to beg, but I would do anything it took to find Lucien and free him.

"You're right that I don't want you to go, but if there's even the slightest chance he's telling the truth, we need that key. Tell me where to meet him."

I shook my head. "I'm coming with you. Jimmy's not going to trust you, and if this is real, I'm the only one he'll talk to."

Angelo growled. "He sure as fuck will talk to me, and he'll give me anything he has."

He was not going without me. "I want to help you save your brother."

"If you get hurt and Lucien finds out it's because I put you in danger by letting you come, my life will be the one that's forfeit."

"Aren't I already in danger? Damian's men have already come to the house, and they took Lucien. I know there are guards, and I know everyone's trying to keep me safe, but I can't stand this. I have to do something."

Angelo stared at me for a few more seconds, then nodded. "Fine. But I'm driving."

I didn't have any problem with that. I told him where Jimmy had told me to meet him. He called Devil on the way but told him to stay put, and we'd check in soon. When we arrived, Angelo refused to make any pretense about me being there alone. He drove around the block, then checked the perimeter of the building before allowing me to get out of the car. He went in first, gun in hand, making sure we weren't about to be ambushed every step of the way.

When he kicked open the door of the back room, Jimmy flinched and nearly fell from the chair where it looked as if he'd been sleeping. He looked even worse than I'd expected. He had a black eye and other bruising on his face. He was cradling one of his arms like it might be broken, and his breath was as wheezy as it had been on the phone. He truly was in bad shape. "You need a doctor, Jimmy."

He shook his head. "If I go to the hospital, they'll find me and finish me off."

Angelo didn't seem to have the same concerns I did. "Tell us what you know right fucking now, or I'm going to finish you off."

"I told you to come alone, Peter."

"I was going to, but Angelo caught me. Now tell us where Lucien is."

Jimmy took a long, rattly breath. For a moment, I thought he might pass out before he gave us the information we needed, but in a barely audible voice, he said. "He's in Damian's basement. He's got fucking cells down there. He's a sick son of a bitch. I think he kept his wife in one for a while."

Angelo stared at him, looking as though he didn't believe

him. "You're saying he keeps prisoners at his house in town? Where his family lives?"

One thing I'd learned was that for most people in Lucien's world, their family home was sacred ground. That's where they kept those they loved under guard, and they didn't bring their business there.

"Not in town. His… big estate."

Angelo glanced at me. "It's not too far from our Weston house."

Jimmy winced as he stuffed his hand into his pocket. Angelo raised his gun, but all Jimmy pulled out was a small key. He held it out to us, and I snatched it before Angelo had the chance.

"What does it open?" Angelo demanded.

"The cell where they're keeping Lucien. I stole it from the man who did this to me. He had it in his pocket."

"Tell me everything else you know about who's guarding my brother, and what their plans are."

Jimmy's eyes fluttered closed, and Angelo shook him. "Wake up. Goddammit." He didn't move.

"Is he…"

Angelo pressed his fingers to the side of Jimmy's neck. "He's still got a pulse for now." He rose and turned toward the door. "Come on. Let's go."

"We're just going to leave him?"

"He betrayed our family, and he played some part in the attack on DiGiulio's. So yeah."

"But he was telling the truth tonight, and he is my cousin."

Angelo sighed and pulled out his phone as he hustled me toward the car. I heard him tell Ralph to come pick up Jimmy, take him to the ER, and make sure nobody offed him before he had a chance to recover.

"Thank you."

"If his information is real, and we find Lucien, then he deserves that much from us."

"And if it's not?"

"Then he won't need to worry about the men who already want him dead. I'll come for him myself."

## 30

## LUCIEN

I passed out at some point while Stefan beat me. I'd tried to fight back at first, and then I just tried not to die. Apparently, I succeeded in that objective. I opened my eyes slowly. Every part of my body ached, but I seemed to be alone in my cell. I needed to get out of there quickly.

I tested the ropes again. Stefan had been too keen on hurting me to bother checking them after he was finished. My struggles had loosened them, not enough to get my hands free but close. If I could fray the rope just a little against the cinder block wall, I would be able to pull them apart enough to free myself. I'd have to find something to pick the lock or summon the strength to overpower whoever brought me food and water, assuming they were going to bother feeding me since they thought I'd be dead soon.

It seemed to take ages for me to scoot across the floor and back myself up to the wall. Every movement was agonizing, but I had to get out of there. I had to get back to my family, to Peter. I needed to make sure they were all safe. They depended on me, and I would not let them down. By the time I wore through enough rope to free myself, my hands were torn and bloody, but I ignored the pain and focused on untying the ropes around my ankles. I stood slowly, pressing my hands against the cold, rough wall as the room spun around me.

*Get it together, Lucien. You can do this.* I took a step away from the wall. My knees wobbled, but I managed to stay on my feet. Each step seemed a little easier. I was nearly at the door when I heard footsteps. Someone slid a key into the lock. Fuck. I was in no condition to fight, but I didn't have a choice.

I picked up the chair Damian had sat in. It was the only thing I had to use as a weapon. Somehow, I found the strength to lift it.

The lock turned.

The door opened slowly.

I tensed, ready to strike.

A man stepped into the room.

I started to swing, then I realized who it was. I almost dropped the chair, but somehow I managed to set it down quietly so it wouldn't alert anyone.

"Peter?"

He closed the door softly behind him. "Oh my God, Lucien. What did they do to you?"

I shook my head. "It doesn't matter. I have to get you out of here. If they find you—"

"Angelo and Devil are here with others. They're going to tear this place apart, but we need to get you to safety. Can you walk?"

"Stefan. He's working for Ricci."

"I know. I saw him take you, and then Jimmy—"

How did he see me? "You were there." Before he could answer, I processed the rest of what he'd said. "Jimmy?"

"It's a long story. We need to go."

Focus. I had to focus. "I can walk, but I don't have a weapon."

Peter held out a gun. "Angelo sent this for you."

"Did he give you one too?"

"Yes, but I don't know how—"

"Point it and shoot. Aim for center mass. You just need to incapacitate someone long enough for one of the rest of us to take them out."

I reached for the doorknob, but the room began to spin again. I'd moved too fast.

"Lucien, are you sure you're all right?"

"I don't have a choice, so I will be. I'll protect you."

"I should be protecting you. You're hurt, and it's my fault. I forgot my phone, and you had to look for me and—"

"When we're all safe, I'll beat your ass for leaving without telling me, but no matter what you did to defy me, this isn't your fault. I was careless. Were there any guards down here when you came to the door?"

He shook his head. "Angelo staged an attack so they'd be distracted."

"Then we need to move quickly before someone catches on." I ignored the fact that my left ankle hurt like fuck. It was nothing compared to the pain in my side. As long as I didn't breathe too deeply, I thought I could make it up the stairs. I had to stop once. For Peter's sake, I pretended I was listening for anyone who might be at the top of the stairs, but my field of vision had begun to narrow. I wasn't sure I could finish the climb without passing out. I reminded myself Peter was counting on me and pushed on. One step at a time.

When we reached the top of the stairs, I motioned for Peter to stay behind me. I had my gun ready, and I prayed I could manage to hit a target. When I opened the door, I was ready to shoot anyone I didn't know.

There was no one there. The house was eerily quiet, but before I could determine the best way to get Peter out of there, I heard my brother shout.

Adrenaline shot through me. I grabbed Peter's wrist, and we ran to where we could take cover and see what was happening outside.

I told Peter to stay put and inched along toward the back of the house where the voices were coming from. A few seconds later, Peter laid a hand on my back as if trying to steady me. He'd completely ignored me about staying put. I needed him to let me handle this. I needed him safe, but I didn't have time to argue. When we got out of there, I was going to make sure he understood that when I told him not to follow me, I meant it.

I heard Damian's voice as we got closer. "Pledge allegiance to me, and you can see your brother again."

Fuck. He was talking to Angelo.

"Bring him to me right now, and we'll sit down and have a talk," Angelo said.

"This isn't a negotiation. My men and I can kill you all now, or you can work for me."

Anger burned through me. How dare that bastard speak to my brother like that. How dare he think he could take all we'd worked for?

"These men aren't loyal to you," Angelo said. "If I take you out, they're not going to give a fuck about your family. They're only in this to advance themselves. Bring me my fucking brother."

They were in a large sunroom. I moved a little closer to the door and leaned out just enough to see how the men were positioned.

Damian had his back to me, and Angelo was facing him. For a second, I thought Angelo might have seen me, but I couldn't be sure. Devil was with him along with Marco. Stefan was standing next to Damian. At least my family knew he was the traitor now. Damian's son was missing, and so was Vinnie. Maybe Vinnie was tracking Mario down.

Angelo was right about the rest of the men I could identify. All they gave a fuck about was themselves. Their allegiance went to any person they thought most likely to win a war. We were going to show them the Marchesis were always winners, then teach them a lesson about doubting us.

It was time for Damian to die. Angelo seemed to be stalling. Was he trying to hold out until Peter freed me because he knew this was my kill? If so, I was damn glad because it would feel good to put him down.

I raised my gun. Peter gasped when I stepped out into the open, but I didn't hesitate. I sent a bullet into the back of Damian's head, and he dropped to the ground.

For a moment, everyone but Angelo, Devil, and Marco seemed stunned. They all stared at each other, trying to figure out what had just happened.

Stefan turned, gun ready. Before I could react, a shot exploded and red bloomed across Stefan's chest. He fell down beside Damian. I turn to see Peter, still holding up his gun with shaky hands. He glanced at me. "I told you I wanted to take care of you."

When no one else moved against us, I laid my hand over his, encouraging him to lower his gun. "You did, baby. That was perfect."

"Th-thank you." All the color had drained from his face. He didn't look any more steady on his feet than I was.

I took his arm and pulled him to stand next to me. A few of Damian's men still had their weapons out, but I didn't think they were a serious threat now.

"This is your one chance to ask forgiveness. After tonight,

consider yourself my enemy." I gestured towards Damian and Stefan with my weapon. "You see what happens to my enemies." One by one, the men gave in to the inevitable, kneeling and begging me to forgive them. They would be punished, but they would live.

If I hadn't had Peter by my side, I'm not sure I could've stayed on my feet long enough to hear their pleas. Between the adrenaline coursing through me and the incredible strength of the man I loved, I stood there through it all, being the leader my family needed.

When everyone but my true allies had been dismissed, all I wanted to do was take Peter home, wrap myself around him, and give him the comfort I knew he needed. He'd never shot a gun before, and he sure as hell had never killed a man. I'd grown up in this life, but this wasn't who Peter was, yet he'd done what he had to for me.

I couldn't go home with him, though. I had to clean up this mess. We needed a story for the police, and I'd have to call my contact in homicide so things could get taken care of quickly. I was also sure Angelo and Devil wanted to know what had happened while I was Damian's prisoner, and we needed to make sure Mario was rounded up along with anyone else who might still be following Damian's agenda.

And while I didn't want Peter to worry over my injuries, I knew I needed a doctor and some time to heal. Comforting Peter—and myself—would have to wait, and it would be best if he went away for a few days, because as much as I wanted to argue otherwise, I was in no shape to keep him safe.

# 31

## PETER

I'd argued with Lucien when he'd said he wanted me out of the city for a few days. I wanted to stay by his side and take care of him while he healed, but weariness and pain showed clearly on his face. I knew arguing with him would make things worse, so I'd given in and agreed to go to a safehouse with Sabrina until he'd regained his strength and his family had made sure all Damian's allies had been tracked down.

He'd said little as we'd ridden back to his house. I knew he was in pain and doing his best to hide how bad it was. He held my hand and that was enough to comfort me as I replayed the events of the evening in my head. I'd killed a man. I'd shot him and watched him die without even trying to see if he could be saved. I was shaken by it, but not as much as I should have been. Stefan would have killed Lucien, and I'd kill him again to save the man I loved.

Lucien had kissed me goodbye before sending me off with his most trusted guards. I'd gone to bed as soon as I reached the safehouse which was hidden deep in a forest, but it had taken me hours before I could fall asleep. I dreamed of

Lucien, confined in a cell, all alone and in pain. I jerked awake just before dawn, terrified that I'd only imagined rescuing Lucien and he was still at Damian's mercy.

Sabrina knocked on my door a little while later to see if I wanted some breakfast. She hadn't come with me the night before, but Lucien had assured me he'd be sending her. I knew I wouldn't get any more sleep, so I agreed to join her.

She made us pancakes and bacon. I thought I wasn't hungry, despite eating little since Lucien had been captured, but once I'd taken a bite, I changed my mind and polished off a tall stack of pancakes.

Sabrina refilled each of our coffee mugs once we'd finished eating. "Now that we've taken care of our hunger and need for caffeine, how are you, really?"

"Better than I would've expected considering what happened."

She smiled. "Good. Angelo told me everything, and you did what was necessary."

"Yeah, I think it was." I decided not to think too hard about my role as a killer, at least not then. "Did you see Lucien last night? How is he?"

She frowned. "In a lot more pain than he's willing to admit and angry with himself for getting captured and needing to be rescued. Angelo and Devil forced him to see a doctor and let them track down the rest of Damian's allies. They promised they'd force him to rest if they had to chain him to the bed."

I could just imagine the trouble he would give them. "Who hurt him? I want to make sure they pay for it."

She smiled. "You sound like one of us now. And you've already made him pay. It was Stefan. Apparently, along with chafing against his father's more conservative ways of running the family, Stefan had resented Lucien for years."

Heat flooded my face. "Only when it comes to protecting Lucien." I thought about that for a moment then added, "I would defend you or Angelo or Devil too if I had to. But that was the only time I'd ever used a gun. I run from danger normally, like I told you."

"You didn't run last night, and Lucien is alive because of it."

She was right. When Lucien had needed me, I'd done what was necessary. "Maybe he's teaching me how to be brave."

"And you're teaching him to remember the man he used to be, and that it's okay to love someone."

"I'm not sure he—" Sabrina raised her brows, and I didn't say anything else.

"Lucien wanted me to tell you that Jimmy was admitted to the hospital overnight. He got rehydrated, and he should make a full recovery. Lucien gave an order for him to be guarded until he's recovered."

"He did that for me? Even though Jimmy went against him?"

"Sometimes even Lucien gives people second or third chances. He's not the monster people believe him to be."

I shook my head. "He's not a monster at all."

"You're right. Sometimes he thinks he is, though, and he doesn't know how to handle it. So he may not say the things you wish he would."

"I know. I've already learned that words can be hard for him, and sometimes he means exactly the opposite of what he says."

She grinned. "My instincts were right. You're perfect for him."

"I want to be."

————

Five days later, I returned home. I truly thought of Lucien's house as my own now. It was late when I arrived, but Lucien was in a meeting. He'd left me a note telling me to wait for him in his room, and he would be there as soon as possible.

I considered going to look for him. I was sure he'd punish me for defying his order, but I already expected him to punish me for leaving my phone on the day he'd been captured and for refusing to hide while he'd confronted Damian and his allies. Every time I imagined how that punishment would feel, heat raced through me, and my cock hardened. I longed to touch him. That had been the hardest part about being separated from him, not having even his platonic touches. Lucien used physical contact to let me know how he was feeling. He'd probably never tell me much about his feelings, but he would show me what he needed with his body.

When I reached his room, I changed into pajama pants and a t-shirt before lying down on his big bed and burying my face in his pillow so I could breathe in his scent. I didn't mean to fall asleep, but I was exhausted. I'd been sleeping poorly since he'd been taken by Stefan.

When I woke up, I was confused about where I was at first. Then I remembered Lucien coming in, curling around me, and kissing my head. Had he really napped with me? Had he really whispered that he loved me, or had that been a dream?

I opened my eyes slowly and saw Lucien standing across the room, talking on the phone.

I sat up and waited for him to end the call. When he did, he didn't rush across the room and pull me into his arms. He reached for the whiskey decanter he always kept on a table near the door and poured a measure for himself. He didn't speak until he'd taken a sip.

"You disobeyed me. I told you to stay put, and you followed me." His hand was shaking. I'd never seen him look so scared, not even when I'd found him in the cell.

"You needed help."

He scowled at me. "You put yourself in danger."

"I did. Knowing you were in danger gave me the courage to help you. I did something I never ever thought I would do, and I did it for you." I climbed from the bed and approached him as I spoke. "Punish me if that's what you need to do, but I would do the same thing again. I will never stand by and let someone hurt you."

I lowered myself to my knees and placed my hands behind my back. I needed him to understand I was here for him, ready to accept what he needed to give.

## 32

## LUCIEN

I looked down at the incredible man who knelt before me, the man I loved. It had been easy to say the words earlier when he was asleep, but now, as he looked up at me expectantly, they wouldn't come. He thought he wasn't brave, but he was incredibly strong, stronger than me. He'd kept it together so well the night he'd rescued me. Even men like me who grew up in a crime family often struggled after their first kill, though not that many of us would admit it. I knew Peter was shaken, but Sabrina had assured me he was handling it well, and he was here. He hadn't tried to run. Instead of being afraid of me now, he was ready to give me what I needed.

He was right; I did need to punish him. I needed him to know how scared I'd been for him. I didn't explain any of that. I just pulled out my cock, stepped closer to him, and slid my fingers into his hair. He opened his mouth, and I fed him every inch of my cock.

He gagged, but he didn't pull away. I held him there, making him submit, because I needed to know he would, and I was as sure as I could be that he needed that too.

He sucked in air when I pulled out, but I only gave him a few seconds before demanding, "More."

Peter brought his hands to my thighs, but I grabbed his wrists. "Keep them behind your back. I'm controlling this. Your mouth is mine."

He looked up at me, eyes dark with need. "Yes, sir." His words might be subservient, but there was a smile on his face that made me think he was humoring me. "Use me, Lucien. I'm here for you."

I drove back into his mouth, making him choke on my cock again before fucking his mouth ruthlessly. He took it all, swallowing around me, sucking and humming. I had to fight to keep from spilling my load. I wasn't ready for that yet.

Finally, I let him go, stepped back, and pulled him to his feet. He drew in ragged breaths while staring up at me.

"Don't ever say you're not brave again."

"Yes, sir."

"You knew I would punish you for defying me, didn't you?"

"Yes, but I also knew you would never truly hurt me."

"You scared me when I couldn't find you, and when I saw you holding that gun... If any of those men had chosen to stand with Damian, I could have been burying you today, not standing here with you." I swiped at my eyes. I was not fucking crying. I grabbed my whiskey and drained the rest of it. "Don't ever scare me like that again."

"I can't promise that because I will always choose to save you if I can, but I can promise that I won't leave you, and I will always obey you when we're together like this."

"Because you want a protector, and you need someone to surrender to?"

Peter shook his head. "No, because I love you."

I closed my eyes for a moment. When I tried to speak, my

voice cracked. Peter laid a finger over my lips. "I know. I knew that day at the barn. Punish me, Lucien. It's what we both need."

I wrapped a hand around the back of his neck and pushed him against the wall. He caught himself on his hands splaying his fingers, then arching his back and wiggling his ass at me. I'd never needed anything like I needed him then.

I grabbed the waistband of his pajama pants and ripped the fabric in two. They slid down his legs. He wasn't wearing anything underneath. I slapped his bare ass hard. He groaned and arched his back more deeply. I smacked him again and again. His ass turned bright red under my blows, and his skin warmed.

"You need this, don't you? You need to remember how important it is to obey me."

"Yes, Lucien. I need to know you care, that you'll always take control, that you'll give us both what we need."

"Fuck right I will." I kept going, spanking him even harder. He whimpered and whined, but he took every blow and begged for more. I wrapped a hand around his cock and stroked him while I brought my blows down on the reddest part of his ass. He thrust into the circle of my fingers, and I used his precum to slick him up so my hand slid more easily along him.

"Please, Lucien. Please. I need to come. Can't stop it."

I wasn't ready for that, so I squeezed the base of his dick and ended the spanking.

I leaned in, mouth right against his ear. "You're not going to come until my dick is buried inside you, until I fuck you deep and hard, filling you up and making you remember who owns you."

"You do, Lucien. I know you do."

I took him by the shoulders and turned him to face me so

our eyes met. "I love you, Peter. I swear to you, I will take care of you, and I will never let you go."

Fucking tears stung my eyes again, but this time it was Peter who reached up and used his thumbs to swipe them away.

"You can be exactly who you need to be with me, Lucien. I love the man you've hidden deep inside yourself, and I love the man who will face down his enemies even when he's bruised and hurting. Any normal man wouldn't have even been able to stand in your condition. I know I'm going to be scared sometimes by the things you do and by the people who threaten you, but I accept you just as you are."

I had to squeeze my eyes shut for a moment and compose myself. Did he have any idea how much those words meant to me?

"Anything you want, I'll give it to you. I'll buy you twenty more horses. I'll give you a new outfit for every day. I'll make sure Lola only makes your favorite meals. I want to shower you with everything. I want to fucking worship you."

"Lucien, all I want right now is your cock inside me."

I growled and scooped him up, carrying him to the bed and tossing him onto the mattress. I stripped myself as fast as I could.

Peter yanked his t-shirt over his head and threw it on the floor. Then he grabbed the lube from the drawer and tossed it to me. I slicked my cock as quickly as I could and lay down beside him, pulling him up until he straddled me. "Ride my cock, Peter. Take it all. Take everything you want from me."

## 33

## PETER

I took hold of Lucien's cock and drew the slick tip over my hole, teasing us both.

Lucien snarled. "I'm giving you a chance to do this, but if I'm not inside you in the next three seconds, I'm going to flip you over and pound your ass until you can't breathe."

"Is that supposed to be a threat? Because you're going to have to do better than that."

He slapped my hand away from his cock and took hold of it himself as he gripped my hip in his other hand. "Fuck me now."

I lowered myself onto him, moving slowly, holding his gaze and loving the heat in his eyes that told me he was as desperate for this as I was.

When he was all the way inside, I circled my hips then arched my back, taking him just a little deeper before leaning down to press my mouth to his as he fucked up into me with shallow strokes.

It felt incredible to kiss him again, but I needed more. I laid my hands on his chest and pushed myself away from him so I could ride him hard and fast. He let me control things for longer than I expected before he took hold of my hips, keeping me still as he drove into me. His cock pressed against my sweet spot, lighting up my whole body and pushing me closer and closer to the moment when I wouldn't be able to hold back.

"So good, Lucien. I want to come. I want to cover you in it."

He groaned, and his fingers tightened on my hips. His grip was almost painful, but I didn't care. There wasn't anything I wouldn't let him do to me right then.

He lifted me off him, and I whimpered. "Don't stop, please. I need this. I need you to take me."

"I know, baby, but I need control. I need this harder and faster. I need to fill you up and mark you as mine."

I scrambled off him and positioned myself on my hands and knees, but Lucien grabbed my hips and dragged me down the mattress. "I want you bent over the end of the bed."

I hurried to obey, then he got behind me and slammed into me, making me cry out.

"Yes," he growled. "That's it. I need to be able to go hard and deep."

Every stroke dragged over my prostate. I was going to come in seconds. I was so stretched, so full. "Going to come, Lucien. I can't hold back."

"Come for me, baby. I want to feel it." A couple more of his rough strokes was all it took. I cried out and cum shot from my cock without Lucien or me ever touching it.

Before I came down from the high of climax, Lucien drove deep, and I felt the hot flood of his cum filling me. It was exactly what I needed from him. A few seconds later, he pulled out. I stayed where I was, enjoying the feel of his cum running down my inner thighs.

"Don't move," he ordered.

He left me long enough to get a washcloth. Then he cleaned me up, and we stretched out together on the bed. I turned to face him, and the raw emotion in his eyes had me drawing in a sharp breath.

"I love you, Peter. I know being with me won't ever be easy for you, but I need you like I need air to breathe."

"I love you too." I knew how hard it was for him to say those words, and I wondered if he knew how much they meant.

"I didn't mean for this to happen. My father loved my mother deeply, and losing her devastated him. I told myself I'd never let that happen to me, but I know that's not what my mother would've wanted, and no matter how much pain he suffered, my father never wished he hadn't met my mother. You are to me what she was to him, the one person that I want to be with forever. The one person I would do anything for."

I stroked his cheek. "Thank you for telling me that, but you don't have to do anything for me. You just have to keep being you and keep loving me."

"I can do that, but I can't stop being a controlling son of a bitch."

"Lucien, if I wasn't okay with that, I would never have fallen in love with you."

He kissed me then, pulling me into his arms and letting me feel all his strength, assuring me he was my protector but also the man who'd made me realize I could be strong.

## EPILOGUE

Lucien

I followed Peter into the barn, grimacing as I looked down at my expensive leather shoes. I was going to have to get some boots and proper clothes for this if he was going to keep insisting I accompany him.

If he ever doubted my love for him, I would just remind him that there was no other person in the world—not my brother, or my cousin, or my father, or my aunt—that I had ever voluntarily walked through horse shit for.

I didn't like horses. I never had. They looked at you in a way that said they were up to something, and the second you got complacent, that's when they were going to fuck you over. I knew that look. Devil wore it most of the time.

I'd been to the barn a few times since the day I'd purchased Clover and Prince for Peter. Each time my beautiful boy had tried to insist I pet the ponies or feed them a treat. I always declined, but I hated the disappointed look on his face. So when he turned to me that day and held out one of the peppermint treats Clover loved, I took it from him. Love makes you do fucking crazy things.

"Let it rest in your palm and keep your hand flat. That way she won't nibble your fingers."

"Why would I voluntarily feed a creature that might bite me?"

Peter rolled his eyes. "She's not going to bite you hard enough to hurt, but she'll have trouble grabbing the treat if you curl up your hand."

I frowned at Peter, not at all sure that was true, but I'd faced down trained assassins, so surely I could let a small pony eat a treat from my hand. I held my hand out where Clover could reach it. She snuffled, and it tickled, but I bit my lip to keep from laughing. When she snatched the treat and pulled her head back, I yanked my hand away. "There. I did it. Are you happy?"

Peter laughed. "I'll be happier when you learn to relax around her, but I'm very proud of you. Good job."

I snarled at him, but Cathy called out to us before I had a chance to say anything else. She was ready to start Peter's lessons.

He'd taken easily to riding. Cathy was amazed at the progress he'd made in only a few lessons. I leaned against the corral fence, not even worrying about it scratching my suit. The things I did for this boy. As I was watching him walk Prince over some low poles, my phone rang. I glanced at it and saw it was Vinnie. I owed him a lot for the help he'd given my family with the Riccis, so I took the call.

"Marchesi."

"Mr. Marchesi, I've confirmed Mario's and Stefan's involvement in the trafficking ring Jimmy mentioned, and..." His voice broke for a moment. "I've also confirmed that

Mario is the man who killed my sister. I want your permission to make the kill."

I wanted Mario for myself, but I couldn't deny Vinnie this right. "Do you know where he is?"

"He fled town, knowing we were on to him for more than what he did to you. Word is he fancied a Caribbean vacation."

"Permission granted. Track him down and eliminate him."

"Thank you, sir."

"Keep in touch, and after you make Mario disappear, take some time for yourself. You've earned it." Once Mario was gone, Elena and her children would be able to return to the city.

"Will do, sir. I appreciate that."

I ended the call and watched the rest of Peter's lesson. After Prince had been brushed and put back into his stall, Peter and I retrieved the picnic basket Lola had packed for us and headed to a secluded spot on the property that Cathy had suggested.

I knew there would be many more challenges to come, but for now, things were quiet in the wake of the war with the Riccis, and I intended to enjoy every moment of time I had to spend with Peter. We ate the finger foods Lola had packed for us, drank wine, and soaked up the sun. I couldn't recall a time when I'd been happier.

When we finished eating, Peter and I lay back and looked up at the clouds. I enjoyed looking for shapes in the sky, something I hadn't done since I was a kid, but after a while, the feel of Peter's warm body pressed against mine made me forget about clouds and start thinking about how much I wanted to take him there under the bright blue sky with the warmth of the sun on our bodies.

I kissed him, gently at first and then harder, my tongue

tangling with his. He returned the kiss with equal passion and pulled me down on top of him. My hand slid down his body to grip his cock and give him long, slow strokes. A few moments later, I unfastened his pants and reached inside, needing skin to skin contact.

"Mmm. Feels so good Lucien. But we shouldn't. Not out here."

"You're forgetting something, baby. I can do anything I want."

Peter started to protest again, but I tightened my grip, and his words turned into a groan. That sound was nearly enough to make me come. I loved how fucking responsive he was, whether he was getting a hand job or steadying himself to take another stroke from my belt.

I released him and sat back. "Turn over on your hands and knees."

"What?" Peter's eyes were wide, his cheeks deeply pink. He looked so damn fuckable.

"I said get on your hands and knees. I shouldn't have to tell you twice. "

"But we're…"

"If you can't obey, you won't get to come."

He scrambled into position. I'd known my threat would work.

"If I want to bare your ass and fuck you right here, then I will goddamn well do it, and I don't care who sees." I yanked his pants down and unfastened my own as quickly as I could. As soon as I'd slicked myself up using the packet of lube I'd taken to carrying at all times, I drove inside him.

I wanted to take things slower, to tease him and toy with him, but this wasn't the place for that. This fuck needed to be fast, rough, and dirty, so that's what I gave him. After we'd both come, I used a napkin to clean us up. When we were fully dressed again, I pulled Peter onto my lap and cupped his face in my hands. "Despite having to feed a horse, this has been the best day I can remember."

He grinned. "Then let's have more days like this."

"We will, baby. We'll have days like this for the rest of our lives."

"You really think you're never going to get tired of me?"

"Tired of you? Not even a chance. And believe me there are still so many things, new things, I want to try with you."

His eyes lit up. "Are you ready to go home? Maybe we could try some of them tonight."

"You're insatiable. That's one of my favorite things about you."

Peter laughed, and I hugged him tight, taking a moment to be thankful he'd come into my life and brought the sunshine with him.

Dear Reader,

Thank you for reading *Lucien*. *The Marchesi Family* series continues with Angelo's story.

Want more sexy contemporary stories? Read *Father of the Groom* and the rest of *Love and Care* series.

I offer a free book to anyone who joins my mailing list. To learn more, go to silviaviolet.com/newsletter. You can chat with me on Facebook in Silvia's Salon, and you can email me at silviaviolet@gmail.com. To read excerpts from all of my titles, visit my website: silviaviolet.com/books.

Please consider leaving a review where you purchased this ebook or on Goodreads. Reviews and word-of-mouth recommendations are vital to independent authors.

Silvia Violet

# ABOUT THE AUTHOR

Silvia Violet writes fun, sexy stories that will leave you smiling and satisfied. She has a thing for characters who are in need of comfort and enjoys helping them surrender to love even when they doubt it exists. Silvia's stories include sizzling contemporaries, paranormals, and historicals. When she needs a break from listening to the voices in her head, she spends time baking, taking long walks, curling up with her favorite books, and hanging out with her family.

Website: silviaviolet.com
Facebook: facebook.com/silvia.violet
Facebook Group: Silvia's Salon
Instagram: @silvia.violet
Bookbub: bookbub.com/authors/silvia-violet

## ALSO BY SILVIA VIOLET

*Ranch Daddy*

*If Wishes Were Horses*

*Lace-Covered Compromise*

*A Chance at Love*

*Coming Clean*

*Revolutionary Temptation*

*Of Hope and Anguish*

**Marchesi Family**

*Lucien*

*Angelo (Coming May 2020)*

**Love and Care**

*Father of the Groom*

*After the Weekend*

*Demanding Discipline*

*Painfully Attractive*

*Hungry (short story)*

**Fitting In**

*Fitting In*

*Sorting Out*

*Burning Up*

*Going Deep*

*Getting Hitched*

**Anticipation**

*Anticipating Disaster*

*Anticipating Rejection*

*Anticipating Temptation*

**Ames Bridge**

*Down on the Farm*

*The Past Comes Home*

*Tied to Home*

**Thorne and Dash**

*Professional Distance*

*Personal Entanglement*

*Perfect Alignment*

*Well-Tailored (A Thorne and Dash Companion Story)*

**Lonely Dragon's Club**

*The Christmas Dragon's Mate*

*The Snow Dragon's Mate*

*The City Dragon's Mate*

*The Island Dragon's Mate*

**Howler Brothers**

*Claiming Bite*

*Bodyguard's Bite*

**Trillium Creek**

*Love at Lupine Bakery*

*Love at Long Last*

Printed in Great Britain
by Amazon